THE ITALIAN VENDETTA

JOEY TORANETTI SERIES

Bob Ieva

DocUmeant *Publishing*
244 5th Avenue
Suite G-200
NY, NY 10001
646-233-4366
www.DocUmeantPublishing.com

DocUmeant Publishing
244 5th Avenue, Suite G-200
NY, NY 10001
Phone: 6462334366

http://www.DocUmeantPublishing.com

©201_ Bob Ieva All rights reserved.
No part of this publication may be reproduced, stored in a retrieval system, or transmitted in any way by any means—electronic, mechanical, photocopy, recording, or otherwise—without the prior permission of the copyright holder, except as provided by USA copyright law.

For permission contact the publisher at publisher@DocUmeantPublishing.com

Disclaimer: All characters appearing in this work are fictitious. Any resemblance to real persons, living or dead, is purely coincidental.

Library of Congress Control Number:

Library of Congress Cataloging in Publication Data
Ieva, Bob.
   Title: The Italian Vendetta: Joey Toranetti Trilogy
   p. cm.
   ISBN 978-1-9378-0181-6

   1Organized Crime—Fiction

   I. Marks, Philip S II. Title
   LCCN:

First Edition

10 9 8 7 6 5 4 3 2 1

Dedication

To Linda, my wife, for supporting me and my endeavor.

Chapter 1

It was the middle of the night; Antonio and Rosa Toranetti were sound asleep. Their infant grandson, Joey, Jr, lay peacefully sleeping in the next room in his crib. Suddenly, a huge bolt of lightning ripped the skies open followed by a clap of thunder that shook the entire house. An ominous wind and torrential downpour obeyed the sky's calling.

Startled by the shrill sound of the insistent ringing of the telephone, Tony leapt out of bed glancing at the clock on the nightstand. It was 3:30 in the morning!

"Hello—?"

"Hello Tony? … This is Augie Tarentina. Is Joey with you?"

"No. Why? What's wrong?'

"Do you know where he is?"

"Yeah, he's on his way to Italy. Why?"

"He left already?"

"Yeah. What's going on?"

"I got a call from my friend, Pasquale Minuto, in Bari, Italy. He told me the Scarapino family is very upset about Joey killing their Godson, Danny."

"What do you mean?"

"From what Pasquale told me, they want revenge."

"Do they know Joey and his wife are on their way to Italy?"

"Yeah; that's why I'm calling. Can you call the hotel and leave a message for Joey?"

"I don't know what hotel he's going to stay in. The limo driver, who knows the area very well, has been instructed to pick out the hotel."

"Why's that?"

That's how Joey set it up with the travel agent."

"Do you know this guy?"

"Yeah, I do. I have his office number, but I think Gino has his home number at the shop. I'll call and have him get the number."

"Good. Call me back at this number." Tony quickly jotted the number down.

Without returning the phone to its cradle, Tony dialed Gino's number. When he answered, without formality, he asked him to get Jim Calloway's home number.

"What's going on, Tony?"

"Augie called and told me that the Scarapino family, in Bari, wants revenge for Danny's killing.

"That's not good. Isn't Joey headed to Italy? I'll get over to the shop and call you from there.

About a half-hour later Gino called Tony with Jim's number and asked, "How can I help, Tony?"

"I'm not sure, Gino. First, I have to locate Joey and Janet."

"Please call me as soon as you know."

"I will, Gino."

Time ticked away, and it was 6 a.m. when Tony hung up. He called Jim Calloway and asked him to find out where Joey was staying and call him back immediately.

Thirty minutes later, Jim called back, "Joey is staying at the Majestic Roma in Rome. Giving him the hotel's number he informed him that Joey was settled into the Junior Suite, room 28."

Immediately Tony phoned the hotel, "Majestic Roma; Phillipe speaking. How may I assist you?"

"Please connect me to room 28."

When Phillipe returned, he informed Tony, "There is no answer sir." Followed quickly by, "May I take a message?"

"Yeah, it's imperative that my son gets this message. Tell him to call his father immediately."

"Are you Mr. Toranetti?"

"Yeah, and it's very important. Just tell him to call me."

"I will give him your message as soon as he returns."

"Thank you, Phillipe. By the way, what time is it there?"

"It is 12:30 in the afternoon here, Mr. Toranetti. I do know that your son made a reservation for lunch at 1:30. So, he should be back within the hour."

"Please watch for him and give him the message just as soon as he comes in."

"I will, Mr. Toranetti."

"Thank you."

Our flight had been unexpectedly delayed at JFK airport. When we finally boarded, it was 7:30 pm. So, by the time everyone was boarded and we took off it was nearly eight o'clock. Our late arrival in Rome was cause for concern being close to ten in the morning. However, after we disembarked in Rome we were immediately shuttled through customs.

Upon arriving at the baggage claim area, we noticed a few drivers standing by with passenger's names on their clipboards. Janet spotted our driver and promptly approached him.

"Welcome Mr. and Mrs. Toranetti. I am Alfredo Cascone. I am at your service for your entire stay while you are in Italy."

"It's a pleasure meeting you, Alfredo. You can call me Joey, and this is my wife Janet." Alfredo was a little over six feet tall and well dressed. He wore a black suit which was obviously tailor-made. I could see the bulge under his lapel. It was the familiar bulge that gave away the fact that he was carrying a piece.

"What hotel do you suggest, Alfredo?"

"I suggest the Majestic Roma Hotel. It is a five-star hotel."

"Okay, let's head over there we're exhausted from the flight."

"If you do not like it, I know some other hotels you might like."

"I'm sure it'll be fine. Our travel agent assured us we would be in good hands with your company."

It took about twenty minutes to get to the hotel. When we arrived I told Alfredo that it looked fine.

"I will wait here until you need me, Mr. Toranetti."

"You don't have to wait, just leave a number at the front desk and I'll call you when I need you."

"Thank you, Mr. Toranetti."

Chapter 1

"Please, call me Joey"

"Yes, Mister … I mean Joey."

We were amazed at the architecture of the hotel. The exterior had an antiquated, but very well-maintained appearance. A doorman, dressed in a black tuxedo with long tails and a top hat, was stationed in front of bronzed revolving doors. When we entered the hotel, we noticed an ornate carving of an angel with wings majestically extending up the wall. As we looked beyond it to the ceilings, we marveled at the hand-painted angelic murals.

The lobby was well-decorated with comfortable chairs and oil paintings of famous landmarks throughout Italy. A small stairway led to the front desk directly in front of us. To our right was another stairway, obviously leading to the guest rooms. We also noticed an attractive dining room to our left and just beyond, a door led to a patio filled with tables protected by large umbrellas.

At the front desk, we were greeted with a welcoming smile by the clerk who introduced himself as Phillipe. As I signed the register he inquired, "What type of room would you like, Mr. Toranetti?"

"Do you have any suites?"

"Yes, sir. The Junior suite is available."

"Great, we'll take that."

"I just need to check the room first to ensure it is ready as you are early for check-in. Would you like some espresso and a pastry while you wait?"

"No thank you."

"I will be right back." Phillipe was gone nearly fifteen minutes. When he returned, he informed us, "Your room is ready, Mr. and Mrs. Toranetti. I will have our bellman show you the way."

When we entered our suite, I tipped the bellman and thanked him. As we glanced around the suite, we were astonished at the spaciousness that greeted us. It was well-adorned with paintings and an elegant king-size bed. The bathroom held a handsome bath tub, two sinks, and a private door to the commode. There were red and white flowers in full bloom carefully arranged in a picturesque vase on the dresser, a bowl of fruit, a bottle of red wine, and two wine glasses. Resting on the wine bottle was a note that read, "Welcome to the Majestic."

After taking in the stunning accommodations, we were no longer quite so exhausted. So, when Janet announced she wanted to visit some of the shops along the boulevard I quickly agreed. But, before we left I called down to Phillipe and asked him to make reservations for lunch at 1:30.

"Would you like to dine in the dining room or on the patio, Mr. Toranetti?"

"The dining room will be fine."

We strolled down the boulevard arm-in-arm, stopping in several elegant boutiques. Janet bought some comfortable shoes and an evening dress. Each purchase we made was carefully wrapped and sent directly to the hotel by the shop owner, which Janet loved, and I was grateful for not having to carry around like her tag along chauffeur.

After a little while I mentioned to Janet, "We need to go back to the hotel if we are going to make our lunch reservations."

"Okay, I'm getting hungry anyway."

Going straight to the hotel hostess stand I informed the hostess, "I'm Joey Toranetti and we have a 1:30 reservation."

"Yes Mr. Toranetti, I will take you to your table. By the way, Phillipe has a message for you at the front desk. He told me to tell you when you arrived that it is very important."

"A message for me?"

"Yes, Mr. Toranetti, I will let him know you have returned."

"Thank you." Puzzled, I looked at Janet and she looked back at me. Phillipe approached our table and told us that my father phoned from the States and that he had been asked to tell us it was important and that you should call him immediately. He then handed me a telephone as he plugged it into an outlet on the floor under our table.

"Thank you, Phillipe."

"I hope it's not Joey, Jr." Janet stated with a tremor in her voice.

"I'm sure it's not honey." I replied as I picked up the receiver.

"How may I assist you?"

"This is Mr. Toranetti, room 28. I would like to place a person-to-person call to New York." I gave her the number and in no time my father's phone rang.

"Hi, Dad. Is Joey okay?"

"Yeah, he's fine."

"Turning to Janet I informed her that Joey was fine." She let out an audible sigh of relief.

"It's you and Janet that aren't."

"What do you mean?"

When my father told me about the Scarapino family, my expression changed and Janet mouthed the words, "What's wrong?"

I held up a finger to gesture to give me a minute as I continued to speak into the phone. "Are they in Rome?"

"We don't know. They are based in Bari, but they could be anywhere. I'll call you back when I have any news."

I told Janet what my father said. Fear washed over her face. "Don't panic, Janet, we just need to work this out."

"How can I not panic, Joey? I'm scared. I really thought all this was over!"

"So, did I honey, so did I." Just then the waiter came over with the menus. "I am very sorry but we can't stay. Thank you." We left and went back to our room where we ordered a light lunch from room service. While we were waiting, I called my father back. "Hi Dad, call Augie and ask him if his friend can come and talk with me."

"Why, Joey?"

"I want to know everything about the Scarapino family. I need to see this man's eyes. As you know, you can tell a lot about a man when you're face-to-face."

"Don't you trust him?"

"I don't know him, Dad. But, I need to get to know him."

"Augie might get offended when he finds out you don't trust his friend."

Chapter 1

"Just tell him, we're on our own because I don't know anyone here. Let him know I need to meet his friend to get to know him personally, so we can map out a plan."

"Okay, Joey, but I think it's best that you call Augie yourself."

"Yeah, you're probably right. Give me his number."

Janet came over tears welling in her eyes, just as room service arrived with our lunch. I knew she was thinking, *when is this going to be over?* I let the waiter in, tipped him, and strode over to Janet. "Listen, I know your upset, but we'll get through this, I promise."

"I know, Joey, I just don't want anything to happen to you."

"You're not going to lose me. I promise. I have to call Augie, then we can talk over lunch."

I called Augie and he immediately understood why and what I wanted and quickly agreed. "I'll call you back and let you know when and where you two can meet. His name is Pasquale Minuto."

Thanks, Augie. I really appreciate your help and understanding. I just need to know more about who I'm dealing with.

Janet and I ate our lunch as we tried to figure out what to do. I wanted her to get on a plane and go back to Brooklyn. But, she flatly refused,

"That's crazy, Janet!"

"I am not leaving and that's final!" I knew it was useless to argue with her.

After we finished lunch, I called the front desk and asked to speak with Phillipe.

"How can I assist you Mr. Toranetti?"

"Did my driver leave a number where he could be reached?"

"Yes, do you need him now, Mr. Toranetti?"

"Yeah, call him and tell him to come to my room as soon as he can."

"I will, Mr. Toranetti."

About twenty minutes later, there was a knock on our door, "Who is it?" I called out.

"It's Alfredo, Joey." I opened the door.

Alfredo entered and asked, "What can I do for you?"

"I need your help. But, before I tell you what I need, I have to ask you something."

"What do you need to know Joey?"

"Why are you carrying a piece?"

"It is actually for your protection. We will be driving around the country in many different areas and you never know what can happen. Would you prefer I didn't carry it?"

"Not at all. Janet and I were just informed by my father in New York that a certain family from Bari is looking for me."

"What family and why?" I explained the situation to Alfredo, figuring he would want nothing more to do with us, and gave him the option of leaving. "I don't know the family but I know of them. I will do whatever I can to assist you."

"I'm going to have two men come to Italy to help. What I want to know is can you get some protection for us, legally?"

"I do have some friends."

"I'm meeting with someone I don't know, but he's a close friend of a friend back in New York. I will let you know soon. In the meantime, please contact your friend for me."

"I have an extra piece in the limo. I can get it for you if you want me to."

"Thanks. That's a good idea." Alfredo left the room and returned in ten minutes with a 9-millimeter, one that I was very familiar with. I called my father and asked him to send Gino and Justin. "Don't tell anyone. I will get them what they need."

A few minutes later Augie called, "Joey, you can meet Pasquale Minuto tomorrow at 1:30 in Campobasso. He'll be at the Ristorante New Charly. Just ask anyone where it is. Pasquale will help you with whatever you need."

"Thank you, Augie. I'll be in touch."

Calling my father, once again, I told him about the meeting. "Dad, tell Gino and Justin if I'm not here when they get there to wait in the lobby. I'll be there as soon as I can."

"Okay. I'll see that they get there tomorrow."

I called Phillipe and asked him to have our driver pick us up at 7:30 a.m. and scheduled a wake-up call for six.

Chapter 2

The next morning, I woke before the wake-up call. As I lay there quietly, so as not to disturb Janet, I thought about what to ask Pasquale. *How do you know the Scarapino family? How did they know I would be in Italy? What can you tell me about them? Where are they now?* I was deep in thought, when Janet stirred. As she nestled in my arms she sleepily asked, "Are you okay, Joey?"

"Yeah, I couldn't sleep. Did I wake you?"

"No. I'm worried about this meeting too."

"I'll call room service, you want anything?"

"Whatever you get is fine."

I ordered cappuccino, croissants, and fruit cups. When I hung up I asked Janet if she wanted to get ready first.

"Might as well, it will keep my mind off things for just a minute or two longer."

Chapter 2

While she was showering, I picked up the piece Alfredo had brought up and checked to see if it was fully loaded and clean. It was well-oiled and ready for use.

Suddenly there was a knock on the door, "Room service." I heard the intruder call through the door. I still had the gun in my hands, so I quickly put it behind my back as I looked through the peep hole in the door. It was indeed room service. "Just a minute," I called back while placing the gun under a cushion on the sofa. I opened the door and the waiter brought in our breakfast. When he left, I thought, *I'm getting paranoid already.*

Janet came out of the bedroom and asked, "Is breakfast here yet?"

"Yeah, it just came." I didn't want her to see I was anxious so I smiled and said, "Smells great too."

We drank our cappuccino, ate our jelly stuffed croissants and talked about the upcoming meeting.

"Joey, do you think Pasquale Minuto will be able to help us?"

"I sure hope so. I have to trust Augie. But once we meet, I'll be able to determine if he is trustworthy or not." It was almost time to leave when I turned to Janet and instructed her, "Don't answer the door or let anyone in while I'm dressing."

What if it's Alfredo?"

"Look through the peep hole first. Then let him in."

"What's going on, Joey?"

"I'm just being cautious. That's all."

At 7:25 a decisive knock on the door announced Alfredo's early arrival. Since it was not yet time, I quickly went to the sofa and grabbed the gun stashed there, "Who is it?"

"It's Alfredo." Looking through the peephole, I saw it was indeed Alfredo, and with a sigh of relief opened the door.

"Hi, Alfredo."

"Good Morning, Joey."

"Do you know where Campobasso is?"

"It is about three hours south of here. Is this where the meeting will take place?"

"Yeah. Have you heard of the Ristorante New Charly?"

"I know exactly where it is."

"Great. We need to be there by 1:30. Based on how long of a drive you said, we should be there in plenty of time. Have you talked to your friend?"

"I have. He said everything will be taken care of today. You will have whatever you need tomorrow morning."

"Thanks. My guys will get here tonight."

Janet walked over, "Joey, can I have a word with you?"

"Sure."

"Privately!" I excused us and we went into the bedroom. Janet turned to me with a concerned look in her eyes, "Why are you so jumpy? Did something happen?"

"Nothing happened, honey. I just don't like being put in this situation when I am in an unfamiliar environment. Not knowing who we're dealing with is frustrating. That's what's making me so jumpy."

"What about Alfredo? Do you trust him?"

"Yeah, I trust Alfredo. I'm just not used to being so vulnerable."

We went back into the living room and I told Alfredo, "Janet's worried because I'm already getting jumpy about this meeting."

15 / Chapter 2

"I noticed that too. But, I totally understand. You're in a strange country and not in your familiar environment. I'm here to protect the both of you."

"Thank you, Alfredo. That means a lot to us. It's time to go."

As we were driving Alfredo asked, "Since we'll be a bit early would you like to see the village of Castel San Vincenzo?"

I turned to Janet, "What do you think, honey?"

"I would love to see it. It might even help take my mind off the situation, at least for a few minutes."

"We came to Italy to see stuff, so why not. As long as we can be in Campobasso by one o'clock, because I need to look around before the meeting." Alfredo gave me a thumbs-up. "Can you tell us more about this area?"

"Sure, Joey, I would be happy to. Castel San Vincenzo is built on the slopes of Mount Vallone. It's in the region of Molise. We will be about forty-five minutes from Campobasso which is the capitol of the Molise region. It has stunning views of the mountainous countryside. There's a commune there called, San Vincenzo al Volturno. It's a historic Benedictine monastery that was constructed by the monks in the eighth century. The medieval monastic center of San Vincenzo al Volturno is located on the Rocchetta plain over-looking a deep gorge cut by the River Volturno. It rests on the edge of the Abbruzzo mountains and has an absolutely spectacular view. We can spend an hour or so and still be in Campobasso in plenty of time for you to check things out."

As we drove to the village we noticed how narrow the roads were. While driving up the hillside we saw a scattering of old stone homes. Alfredo found a parking lot for tourists and parked in one of the few remaining spots. Exiting the car we spotted a group of tourists walking around, so we stayed close enough to be able to hear what the guide was saying. He informed us that in 881 the abbey was destroyed by a band of Arabs. Some years later the monks that survived the attack started to rebuild the abbey. The abbey which we were walking through now has been rebuilt again after it was destroyed in the Second World War.

Janet was astonished with the history and the views. "Imagine the beauty of this abbey when it was originally built!"

"Yeah, it's a shame what people do out of jealousy and hate." I looked at my watch and motioning to Alfredo. "We better get going if we want to get to Campobasso by one o'clock."

After we had driven for about forty-five minutes Alfredo announced, "We're entering the region of Molise and the province of Campobasso. We'll be at the Ristorante New Charly in about fifteen minutes."

I knew we had plenty of time to look around. As we pulled into the parking lot of the restaurant I noticed that there were only two other cars there. The restaurant was surrounded by a six-foot, black, wrought iron fence. We entered through the open gate. On the other side of the gate was a beautiful cobblestone pathway. The name Charly was written on a plaque on the pathway. On the left was a two-foot-high wall constructed of enormous stones. Behind the wall were some small bushes and trees. To our right a row of matching one-foot-high stones ran along the whole pathway separating more bushes and trees from our path. As we followed the cobblestone pathway we came to a patio that led to the entrance to the restaurant.

    The front doors of the restaurant were shaped like the archway we had passed under. The upper part of the doors had a half-moon shape and each door came to a point where they perfectly matched the archway. As we entered the restaurant we noticed that there were ten tables, all were covered with white linen tablecloths, with matching cloth napkins at each place setting. I couldn't help but notice two men at a table by the wall on the right. I didn't see anyone behind the bar on the left. There was a cooking station with a large open pizza oven, but no one manned the station. In the middle of the restaurant there was a man seated alone at a table for four. It was obvious he was sitting there so he could observe whoever entered the restaurant.

    I gave Alfredo a look that I could tell he recognized right away, "Be ready for anything." I turned to Janet, "Stay behind Alfredo and me." I slowly walked over to the man sitting alone at the table. "Are you Pasquale Minuto?" I asked as I approached the lone man.

    "Yeah." He stood up, "You must be Joey Toranetti," he said as he took my hand and shook it firmly. He had a genuinely firm grip, was my height, and approximately Augie's age. You could tell that at one time this man was built very well. The way he handled himself and talked reminded me of home.

I have to say Mr. Minuto, I'm not completely comfortable right now. Who are the two men at that table over there?" I asked nodding my head in their direction.

"They are friends. I have been followed ever since I talked to Augie. They're here to protect me and you. Who are the people with you?"

"This is my wife, Janet and my friend and driver, Alfredo. Alfredo is here to protect us. Were you followed today?"

"I don't think so. We were very careful. I'm sure you have questions. So, ask away?"

"First I have to ask, have you always lived in Italy?"

"No, I was born and raised in Brooklyn, but had to leave for certain reasons. I've been here for twenty years now."

"So, that explains how you know Augie?"

"Yeah, Augie and I grew up together."

"Okay. How do you know the Scarapino's?"

"Let's just say I'm a distant relative. I knew Danny, their godson. As you know, Danny was a bad seed. He would lie to your face and kill you in an instant, for no apparent reason."

"If his family knows that why do they want to avenge his death?"

"Danny gave the family high hopes of going to America and taking over Brooklyn. You see, his family couldn't get papers to go to America because they had felony records. Danny told them that with the people he knew he could get them forged papers. Once in America they could make a fortune in Brooklyn."

Chapter 2

"Wow. No wonder he wanted to destroy me and my family. Why are you willing to help me?"

"I heard a lot of good things about you from Augie. That's why I called him."

"Do you know where they are now?"

"Not yet. I am working on it."

"Do you know how they found out we were coming to Italy?"

That's easy Joey. Someone close to Danny, someone in your organization, told them."

I started looking around and still didn't see anyone at the bar or kitchen area. "Where are all the employees?"

"I know the owner well; he's allowing me to have a meeting here. He doesn't open to the public until four anyway."

All of a sudden I saw three men come in from the back with guns drawn. In one fluid motion the two men at the table by the wall jumped up, pulled out their guns and yelled, "Pasquale!"

I yelled to Alfredo, "Get her out of here." Alfredo shot one of the three men as he was steering Janet out of the restaurant. One of Pasquale's men went down. I was already shooting when I noticed Pasquale was having issues with his gun, so I jumped in front of him and shot the man coming at us. The second man with Pasquale killed the third man.

"Are you okay, Pasquale?" His friend asked.

"Yeah, thanks to Joey and you. My gun jammed. How's Roberto?"

"He didn't make it."

"Your friend, who owns this place, is going to be upset with all the damage."

"Don't worry Joey. I'll take care of everything. Just make sure your wife is okay."

"What about you and your friend here?"

"We'll be fine. We've already planned for something like this. But, thank you for your concern."

"Here's the number of my hotel if you need me."

"Thank you, Joey. If I need you, or find anything out, I'll call."

With that I walked out to the parking lot. Alfredo was standing outside the car with his gun by his side. I walked to the car looked in and saw Janet lying on the back seat. I got in the car. "Are you okay honey?"

"I'm fine, just scared. Are you okay?"

"I'm okay. Let's get out of here."

"Are we going back to the hotel?"

"Yeah, straight back to the hotel."

Chapter 3

We arrived at the hotel just before six. Gino and Justin were sitting on a couch when we walked in. "Hi Gino, Justin." We hugged each other.

"Gino, Justin, meet my friend Alfredo." They shook hands and Alfredo welcomed them. Gino, this is Alfredo's number. If you need anything call him."

"Will do, Joey."

"How was your flight?

"It was good but long. Hi, Janet."

"How are you, Gino?"

"I'm good. This is my friend Justin"'

"Nice to meet you Justin."

"Did you guys have to wait long?" I asked.

"About an hour or so. Hope your meeting went well Joey"

"Kind of. We can't talk here. Let's take a walk outside." We walked away from the hotel and I told them about the shooting.

So, it appears Pasquale's trustworthy?"

"Very much. The hardware will be here tomorrow. Have you had dinner yet?"

"No, not yet."

'Let's go to the dining room. Alfredo, will you join us?"

"Thank you for asking, but I have to leave. If you need me just call."

"Are you sure you can't join us?"

"Yes, I'm sure."

"Okay, talk to you later," When we approached the hostess I said, "We don't have a reservation. "How long of a wait for four?"

"No wait sir, I have a table for four. I will show you to it."

"Thank you. What's your name?"

"Carmela. Genevieve will be your server."

"Thank you very much Carmela." I slipped her a twenty.

Our server came over, and we ordered drinks and appetizers.

When the drinks arrived I made a toast, "To your safe arrival. Salute" After a few minutes we were ready to order. When the waiter returned, we leisurely ordered our meals and wine and chatted about what to do about the situation. It was agreed the best course of action would be to take one day at a time.

After our meal was over we strolled over to the front desk. "Now, let's get you checked in.

"I need a room for my friends."

"I do have a room near yours, Mr. Toranetti, but it isn't a suite."

"That's fine. Have the bellman take them to their room? What's the room number?"

"It is 33. How long will they be staying Mr. Toranetti?

Chapter 3

"I'm not sure, maybe a week. Gino, our room is 28. When you're settled in, join us in our suite."

While we waited for Gino and Justin I called my father, "Hi Dad. How's Joey Jr. doing?

"He's doing well. What's going on there?"

"I met with Augie's friend Pasquale. Turns out he's legit. He told me someone in our organization told them I was coming to Italy." I then proceeded to tell him about the shootout.

"Are Gino and Justin there yet?"

"Yeah. We're waiting for them to get settled in. Look, find out who was close to Danny and let me know. I have to go. Give little Joey a hug and kiss from us."

Gino and Justin arrived about twenty minutes later. Just as they sat down my phone rang, "Hello, hello." There was no answer.

I looked at Gino, by the look on my face he knew something was up. "What's wrong?"

"I'm not sure. Get Janet out of here. Get out of the hotel and call Alfredo. Janet." I yelled out, "go with Gino."

"What's wrong?"

"Just go with Gino. Now! There's a back exit just past your room Gino. Go!" As they left I called Phillipe, "Who called my room?"

"Two men saying they were the police. But, I did not believe them. They are on their way up."

I hung up, walked to the peep hole, and watched. When I saw them I knew they weren't cops. I walked to the couch and laid my jacket on it to look like I was sitting there and promptly I went into the bedroom. Suddenly I heard the door crash against the wall and then gunshots. They were shooting my jacket. I ran out of the bedroom, they turned, and I shot both of them in the head.

I phoned down to Phillipe, "You're right, they weren't cops. Call the police."

When the Polizia Municipale arrived, they looked at me and asked, "What happened?"

"They tried to kill me!"

"Why?"

"I didn't have time to ask. I was too busy protecting myself."

"We will need you to come to headquarters."

"Of course. Am I under arrest?"

"Not at this time. We just need to know what happened." As we were leaving the hotel I saw Gino in Alfredo's car.

We arrived at the Questura, where I was taken to a small room, like the interrogation rooms in Brooklyn. I wasn't surprised. A few minutes later the cops that brought me to the station came in. A man in a suit followed.

"I am Inspector Falcone. Tell me exactly what happened in your hotel room, Mr. Toranetti."

"I was in the bedroom when I heard this crash, then lots of gunshots. I came out and saw them shooting at my jacket."

"Where did you get the gun to kill them?"

"They must have dropped it breaking down my door. So I just picked it up and protected myself."

"Am I supposed to believe that?"

"Inspector, I don't care what you believe. That's what happened." The inspector gave me a look like he wanted to smack me.

"Why would they try to kill you?"

"How should I know? All I know is that they shot up my favorite jacket."

"Who were they?"

"I don't know; I've never been here before. I don't live here. My wife and I are here on vacation." The inspector just stared at me. "Am I under arrest?"

"Not at this time."

"Good, I'm leaving."

"Do not leave town. And, I need your passport."

"I wouldn't dream of it. I handed him my passport and left the Questura. When I went outside I found a phone, called Alfredo, and had him pick me up.

As I got into Alfredo's car I asked, "Where's Janet?"

"She is at my cousin's house with your friends. Do you think they were from the Scarapino's family?"

"Yeah, who else could it be?"

"How did they know you were at the hotel?"

"I'm thinking we were followed from the restaurant. Did you notice anyone?"

"No. I would have said something."

"When can we get the hardware and the papers?"

"I can get them now."

"Great. Drop me off at your cousin's first."

We arrived at Alfredo's cousin's place in a matter of minutes. I walked in and Janet came running over and hugged me really tight. "Are you okay, Joey?"

Yeah, I'm fine. How about you?"

"I'm good now. I was afraid I lost you."

"I know, everything's fine. You're safe and that's all that matters. Right now, I need to talk to Gino and Justin."

Gino came over and asked, "How did they know?"

"I don't know. Alfredo is picking up what I ordered and bringing it here. Where's his cousin, I want to thank him?"

He's out of town. Alfredo's watching his house."

"We need to get our stuff out of the hotel and find a safe place to hold up."

Just then Alfredo came back with our equipment. "Here are your legal papers and hardware. My father told me to call if we need him."

"I don't want to get your father involved in this. He could get hurt."

"My father knows a lot of people. Just like yours Joey. How do you think I was able to get this stuff?"

Chapter 3

"Who's your father?"

"Giuseppe Caladessi. He doesn't like the Scarapino's."

"How does he know them? They're in Bari."

"Like I said, he knows many people."

"Okay, I get it. Tell him thanks; we'll call him, if needed. For now, we need to pay our bill at the hotel and find a safe place to stay."

"You can stay here, Joey. I will handle your bill and get your stuff. You can't go near the hotel."

"Alfredo, may I ask you why your last name is different than your father's? I will understand if this is too personal."

"I will be happy to tell you. My parents and Giuseppe were very close friends, so we were always over at Giuseppe's house. When I was six years old my parents had a fatal car accident. So, when Giuseppe took me in and raised me as his own I started calling him papa. But, he wanted me to keep my father's name so the Cascone name would carry on.

"Thank you for sharing that. I am sure it couldn't have been easy losing both your parents at such a young age. You're lucky to have had Giuseppe as a father figure. I can see how close you both are. Now, just one more question, how did we get so lucky as to get you for a driver?"

"Your travel agent called my father and asked him to take good care of you. So, here I am."

"That's amazing. I had no idea. Can your father reach Pasquale?"

"I'll ask. Why do you want Pasquale?"

"I need to know how these men found us."

"I'll let you know. Rest up and we will talk in the morning."

"Where're you going?"

"Home. You can protect my cousin's house." He said with a wink." See you in the morning."

I laughed, "We'll try not to make too big of a mess."

Chapter 4

Alfredo arrived the next morning with a bag full of croissants and cappuccinos. There was enough for an army.

"Good morning Alfredo, thanks for thinking of us."

"Good morning, Joey. I was afraid when you looked in the cupboard you would find them bare."

"We had noticed." We all laughed. "Have you spoken to your father?"

"Yes, he is looking for Pasquale as we speak."

Janet looked up and asked, "Can we tour Rome today?"

"I don't know honey. What do you think Alfredo?"

"With all of us together, I don't think it will be an issue."

It was decided. Janet wanted to see the Vatican. So, we finished breakfast, dressed and left for our tour. On our way to the car Alfredo told us to keep our eyes open for anything that looked suspicious.

We arrived thirty-five minutes later in Rome and we were amazed at the size of the crowds. As we drove Alfredo explained that; "Vatican City is its own country within Italy. He explained that it has over 900 full-time residents. The Pope and the residents have diplomatic immunity if they live in the Vatican. He asked, "What would you like to see?"

I made it very clear. "I'm not standing in these lines!"

"Don't worry, as a tour company, I have special authorization for my guests. We get ahead of the lines. So, Janet what would you like to visit?"

"I have always wanted to see the Sistine Chapel."

"Okay, that's not far from here. So, you want to see Michelangelo's paintings? You will be amazed at his work."

When we walked into the Sistine Chapel, I was indeed amazed. I looked at Janet, and could see she was awestruck also. "Isn't this beautiful? Look at the paintings on the ceiling!" Janet blurted out. "I can't imagine how he painted that." She said pointing up.

"They used wooden scaffolding designed by Michelangelo himself. He hooked himself to the walls with brackets." Alfredo conveyed, "Many people think he painted while on his back, but actually, he painted these beautiful paintings standing up and reaching up with his hands. It took Michelangelo several years to paint the ceiling. He started in 1508 and didn't finish until 1512. This has become the cornerstone art- work of the Renaissance."

"Wow! Isn't this astonishing, Joey?"

"Yeah, simply astounding. Kinda sounds like he had something to prove."

Chapter 4

"That is very true Joey" Alfredo commented. "He was known as a great sculptor, not a painter. He was commissioned by Pope Julius II in 1508 to repaint the vault, or ceiling, of the Chapel. It was originally painted as golden stars on a blue sky. Many of the great artists said he would fail."

"He definitely showed them."

Alfredo looked at his watch, "We need to head back to the house. It's getting late."

We all agreed. As we were walking to the car I noticed Alfredo kept looking behind us. "What's wrong?"

"I think we're being followed. I see the same person every time I look around."

"Let's take a right on the next block."

We turned the corner; Alfredo looked back, "He's still following us."

"Turn and walk towards him." We turned and headed for the person following us. He walked into a store. As we passed, he came back out; and started to follow us again. I stopped, turned and ran at the man, grabbed him and put him against a wall, "Why are you following us?"

"I'm a polizia municiple, the Inspector told me to follow you."

I looked at Alfredo, "He's a cop. Officer do you realize people tried to kill us once already. You could have been another killer for all I knew."

"Yes, I do realize that, Mr. Toranetti. But, the inspector wanted to know where you were going at all times."

"Have you been following me since my questioning?"

"Yes."

"Well, I have to say, you are pretty good. Obviously, you know where we live. That's where we're going. So, you can stop following us. I turned to Alfredo and asked, "Where are we going to eat?"

"A little restaurant by the house."

"Tell the officer where it is. Would you like to join us for dinner officer?"

"No, thank you. I will go back to headquarters and tell the inspector where you are."

"What's your name?"

"My name is, Domenico Alissi."

"Okay Officer Alissi, tell the inspector we aren't leaving town, we're only touring Rome. Remind him that, as I told him, we're here on vacation."

After dinner we returned to the house. When we entered, the phone was ringing. Alfredo answered, "Hello, this is Alfredo. Oh, hi papa."

"I have located Pasquale."

"That's great. When and where can we meet?"

"I will bring him to you. Tomorrow morning at ten o'clock."

"We will be waiting. Thank you."

As soon as Alfredo hung up I asked, "Has your father found Pasquale?"

"Yes. They will be here in the morning."

"Great. Maybe he can shed some light on where the Scarapino's are." I turned to Janet, "Honey, you really need to go home."

Chapter 4

"I'm not going home, Joey. I already told you, I'm staying right here with you. Please don't ask me again." I resigned myself to the fact she wouldn't leave. "Justin, Gino, stay close to her from now on."

"We will, Joey."

With that said we all decided to get a good night sleep.

The next morning Alfredo picked up another batch of croissants. When he returned, he made two pots of espresso, and had the table set for our guests. I walked into the kitchen, "Well, you've been busy."

"I just want to make sure everyone will be comfortable."

As I looked at the settings on the table I questioned, "How many people will be here?"

"Counting us, there are nine, with Pasquale's bodyguard." Janet, Justin, and Gino came in and each grabbed a cup of espresso. Alfredo quickly made another pot. It was nearing ten o'clock and Alfredo was pacing back and forth, nervously fixing the napkins, and adjusting the silverware.

"Something wrong, Alfredo? You seem a bit nervous."

"I get like this when my father's around."

"Why?"

"He likes everything perfect."

"Everything is perfect."

"I know, I'm just making sure." At that moment, the doorbell rang. Alfredo answered it, "Ciao papa. Joey, this is my father Giuseppe Caladessi."

Giuseppe was about six feet tall, husky, with grey hair, blue eyes, and a confident demeanor. With a firm shake of my hand I offered, "It's a pleasure meeting you, Mr. Caladessi."

"My son has told me that you are a stand-up guy, Mr. Toranetti."

"Call me Joey."

"You may call me Giuseppe."

We all introduced ourselves. Extending my hand, I went over to Pasquale. "Hi Pasquale, how are you?"

"Not that great Joey. I have had to hide from the Scarapino's. Thank God for my body guard Rico; he's outsmarted them twice already."

"I'm glad you're okay. Come, let's all sit and have something to eat." We sat, and enjoyed the croissants, and espresso. After we ate and chatted a while, I stated, "We need to help each other, Pasquale. We need to end this. Who are the leaders of this family?"

"The head of the family is Angelo Scarapino and his wife, Angelina. She is the nastiest. Why, what are you thinking?"

"I would like to set up a meeting with the Scarapinos."

Giuseppe turned to me and voiced his concern, "You can't reason with these people. The Scarapinos made up their minds, they want you dead, and will not stop until that happens."

"What do you suggest we do?"

"Go back to New York"

"I'm not going to do that. I will settle this, one way or another."

"That's crazy. You will get yourself and everyone else killed."

"That's not going to happen. I will find a way to end this."

Chapter 4

"Well, my son is not getting involved"

"That is for me to decide, papa. I know how much you despise the Scarapinos. They are nothing but killers. Besides, you always said 'One day they will be sorry.' Well, now is that day."

Giuseppe looked at his son, then at everyone else and replied, "I guess I'm getting too old for this stuff, you're right mio figlio. I'll help where I can."

"Thank you, papa, The Scarapinos think they can do whatever they want. They must be stopped!"

"You do realize this could turn into an all-out war?"

I turned to Giuseppe and said, "Communication is the key. We must have a meeting with the Scarapinos, and try to settle this. I don't want to start a war either."

"I think I can set that up. There's one person in the family that doesn't like the way they run things."

"Who's that?"

"Carmine."

"How does he fit into the family?"

Pasquale chimed in, "He's the youngest son and wants nothing to do with the business."

"Does Carmine have any say in the family business?"

"He's their son, they will hear what he has to say. But, that doesn't mean they'll listen."

"It won't hurt to try. Giuseppe, what do you think?"

"I'm with you. I'll call and ask for his assistance."

"Okay, let's set up the meeting in a busy restaurant that has a private room."

"Okay. I'll let you know when and where, Joey."

"Great. If there's an issue, we'll figure another way."

"I'll call you soon. Pasquale, you and Rico will stay at my place."

"Thank you, Giuseppe. We really appreciate it."

After everyone left, Janet asked, "Is it safe? Can we continue to tour Rome?"

"I don't see why not. What do you think, Alfredo?"

"If we all stay together it should be safe enough."

"Great. Where would you want to go, honey?"

Janet turned to Alfredo, "Let's go to a cafe, shops, and then out for dinner."

"I'll take you to the best places."

We all piled into Alfredo's car and drove toward Vatican City. The first place we stopped was a café just outside of the city. They had actual coffee and the best pastries we ever tasted. Janet looked over at me and declared, "We need these in Brooklyn!"

"Let's bring the chef back with us and open a pastry shop." I blurted out sarcastically.

"Very funny! You can be replaced." We all started laughing, all except for Janet.

"I was only kidding, honey. Sorry."

She looked at me and burst out laughing, "I got you! I knew you were kidding."

Alberto jumped in, "How about some gelato?"

"Yeah!" we all chimed in at once.

Chapter 4

"It's right across the street and they have the best gelato in Rome."

"What makes it the best?" I asked.

"Well, it is super smooth and creamy with an intense flavor. There are a lot of flavors to choose from, but the chocolate is fantastico."

We all ordered the flavors of our choice, but when Janet tasted the chocolate, she whispered, "Can we live here, Joey?"

"If it's that good, maybe we can have it shipped to us. This almond flavor is out of this world. Alfredo, do you think they will ship to Brooklyn?"

I'm not sure. You can ask, but I don't think they will, or even can."

"Wow, that's the best gelato I've ever tasted." Everyone agreed. "We'll come back and ask another day. Why don't we go back to the house and relax for a bit?"

"That sounds good, Joey. It's been a long day. I think we're all exhausted."

As we were walking to the car, Alfredo mentioned, "Officer Alissi is following us again."

"I know; I saw him a few times. He really isn't very good, but he's trying. We just have to accept it, for now."

"Okay. Does everyone else know he's on the job?" Alfredo asked.

"I'm sure they do. I told them we would be followed. So, let's not worry about it for now. When we need to lose him we will."

Gino walked up to us and said, "I'm sure you saw the cop following us again."

"Yeah, don't worry about him."

"Well, he just got into that black sedan across the street. There are two or three men in it. I don't think they're all cops."

I looked across the street, just as the car doors opened. Four men in long, tan rain coats got out. They were all big, but heavy, and couldn't move fast. You could see their heat sticks poking out from the bottom of their coats. We were a considerable distance from them. "You're right, Gino, they're not cops."

"Joey, if we get back into the crowds we can separate and meet at the pastry place in twenty minutes."

"That's a good idea. Janet, stay with Gino."

"Where are you going?"

"They want me. I'll lead them away from you."

"That's crazy. They'll kill you."

"They'll have to catch me first." I called out over my shoulder as I took off running. When I looked back, I saw the men get back into the car and drive towards me. I ran into an alley, where there was an open door a few feet ahead. Inside was a stairway that looked like it led to the roof. I ran up the stairs. At the top was a door. I opened it and it was the roof. I ran to the edge and as I looked down, I saw the men were just getting out of their car. They were looking all around for me. They never once looked up. After a little while they retreated to their car and drove away. I waited a few more minutes, walked down to the street, headed to the pastry shop, and met up with everyone there.

Janet ran over, hugged me, then punched me in the chest. "Don't ever do that again!"

Chapter 4

"I had to steer them away from you, honey. They're gone now. Since that cop was with them they probably know where we're staying. Alfredo, do you have any suggestions?"

"My father has a villa not far from here. We can go there for now. I will call him when we get there."

Chapter 5

Giuseppe's home was in the suburbs of Rome. It was on Palatine Hill, one of Rome's famous hills in Balduina, situated just above Prati and the Vatican. It was a two-level building, like a town house. The rooms weren't very large, but not as small as in an apartment or condominium. In the dining room, there was a beautiful, oval oaken table that had eight exquisite high back chairs surrounding it. This room was considered the most important room. It is where the whole family congregated for meals, meetings, and get-togethers. Giuseppe showed Pasquale and Rico to a room on the second floor that they could share. "It isn't much but it will do."

"Thank you, Giuseppe." Pasquale remarked, "This is very kind of you."

"Settle in and then come downstairs to the dining room. We'll figure out what to say to Carmine."

The two men came down about twenty minutes later. "Are you all settled in?"

"We are."

"Good. Let's get down to business. Pasquale, do you think Carmine is our best bet?"

"Yeah, Giuseppe. He loves his parents and wants nothing to happen to them, but he wants nothing to do with their lifestyle."

"I met him a long time ago and got the same feeling. He gave me his number in case I ever needed him. I'll reach out to him."

Giuseppe called Carmine, "Hello Carmine, this is Giuseppe Caladessi, we met awhile back. I'm calling because I need your help. Well, we need to sit down with your father and mother. Yes, we need to discuss the situation with Joey Toranetti. I know they're determined, but do they really want to go to war over this? Okay, talk to them and call me back."

"Is he going to try, Giuseppe?" Pasquale asked.

"Yes; and I hope he succeeds, for all our sakes."

Just then the phone rang, "Hi, Alfredo." Giuseppe listened intently and commented, "Is everyone okay? Good, I'll have their belongings picked up and brought to you. I have talked to Carmine; he will try to set up a meeting. Talk to you soon."

"What happened?" Pasquale questioned.

Giuseppe told them of the attempted attack outside Vatican City. "They are safe; I will have two of my men join them."

When we arrived at the villa, Alfredo told us that his father built this home as a retreat from life in the city. "He had it built to his specifications. He always wanted a garden, grass, and a comfortable place to relax. He also had a secret escape passageway built under the villa."

"Why a secret passageway?" I asked.

"Occasionally, a war breaks out between the families. So, he wanted a way out if they came here."

"That makes sense. Always be prepared."

As we drove up to a wrought iron gate that stood about ten feet high, we were rendered speechless by the beauty of the design on the gate. It didn't have a crest or a name, just handsomely shaped scrolled bars. As the gate opened we were greeted by a view that was absolutely stunning, lush trees, perfectly trimmed bushes, and a magnificently manicured green lawn. It reminded me of Arthur's home in Miami. I looked up at the stone walls and saw cameras everywhere. As we exited Alfredo's car we stepped onto a slate pathway that led to the entranceway. The edges of the pathway were lined with red bricks that were bolstered to the path. On the right and the left of the path were stately, perfectly shaped, dark green hedges.

"This is amazing. Do you come here often?"

Yes, I do. Let's go inside."

We entered the villa and strode across highly polished, light wood floors that led to the family room. This room was decorated with contemporary furniture. There was a leather sofa and two leather chairs that looked very inviting. A large stone wall covered the opposite side of the room and at the base of the wall was a large fire place. Above the fire place was an ornately carved, wooden mantel. Of course, Janet wanted to see the kitchen, so, our host graciously opened the separating door and we were amazed at the enormity of it compared to ours. It held a huge refrigerator, built into a wall, with a stove and oven that looked like it came out of a commercial kitchen. On the other side of the kitchen was the dining room. The table was not enormous, but sat eight guests. In the rear of the villa were a mixture of bedrooms, library, den and a bathroom. Each of the four bedrooms had their own bathroom and fireplaces.

"This villa is outstanding."

"There is a special room I haven't shown you yet. Come with me." We followed Alfredo. He opened the door and there were all the security monitors for the entire villa. "What do you think?"

"This is stupendous, just exactly what we need, a perfectly secure place."

"My father is sending two of his men to help us and to monitor the cameras."

"I know we'll be safe here. Don't you agree, Janet?"

"I'm still in shock at this amazing place. I agree, we'll be fine here."

"Alfredo, when will the men get here?"

"Very soon, Joey. I'll watch for them from this room. In the meantime, there's food and beer in the refrigerator and liquor in the den. Help yourselves."

While we waited for Giuseppe's men I asked Gino, "Do you think that cop had it in him to betray his uniform?"

"No, I think something happened for him to give us up."

"Me to. Let's ask Giuseppe to pick him up and find out."

Alfredo came out and informed us, "They're here and my father is with them."

"Great, we can ask him now."

"Ask my father what, Joey?"

"About the cop that's helping the Scarapinos." Giuseppe and his friends entered the villa, Giuseppe introduced us, Adamo, Dario, this is Joey, Justin, and Janet. These men were huge, not fat, just big. You could tell they weren't afraid of anyone. We shook hands and said hello. The two men went straight to the security room. I walked over to Giuseppe and asked, "Can you pick up the cop that was following us?"

"What is the officer's name?"

"It's Domenico Alissi. He works with Inspector Falcone. He assigned Alissi to follow us."

"I know the Inspector. I'll get Alissi's address and have a talk with him."

"Great. Let me know what he says."

Janet came out of the kitchen and said, "I made spaghetti with garlic and oil and a salad. Come and eat before it gets cold."

I asked Giuseppe to join us, while Janet took two plates to the men in the security room.

We enjoyed our meal, a couple of beers and some wine. Giuseppe rose, as he said, "Thank you for dinner, I will see Falcone in the morning. Get a good night's sleep. It's going to be a long day tomorrow."

Chapter 6

The next morning Giuseppe walked into the Questura, went up to the desk and asked, "May I see Inspector Falcone?"

"Well, well, if it isn't Mr. Giuseppe Caladessi. What brings you here?"

"I just told you. Now, is he here or not?"

"I'll tell him you're here."

A few minutes later the inspector came out and extending his hand said, "Mr. Caladessi, pleased to see you. Come into my office." We entered his office and sat down. "What brings you here, Giuseppe?"

"I need to talk to one of your officers."

"Who might that be?"

"Officer Alissi."

"Why him? I don't see what he could have done."

"Do you know Joey Toranetti, Inspector Falcone?"

"Yes I do, why?"

"Well you had Officer Alissi tail him. "

"Yes, I did. He killed two men in his hotel room."

"The way I hear, it was in self-defense."

"I told him not to leave the country. I'm just making sure he doesn't."

"He gave you his passport. So, you already know he isn't going anywhere. Now, I need to speak with Officer Alissi."

"He's not here. He took a few days off."

"Where does he live?"

"I can't tell you that and you know it!"

"I know. But, you will. Right Inspector?"

"Okay, I don't want any trouble from you. Here is his address. Now please leave. I have work to do."

"Thank you. I really appreciate it. Have a pleasant day." Giuseppe walked out and headed to Officer Alissi's home.

When Giuseppe arrived, he knocked firmly on the door. Officer Alissi jerked it open, "Where are they?"

"Where are who Domenico?" The scene that lay before Giuseppe looked as if a hurricane had blown through the villa. The couch was on its side; the coffee table was busted, even the television was destroyed. "What happened here?"

"Never mind, I thought you were someone else."

"Did you think I was part of the Scarapino family?"

"Who are you?" I could see the nervous look in his eyes, he is definitely afraid of something.

"I am Giuseppe Caladessi. I am here to help you."

Chapter 6

"What makes you think I need help?" He started to perspire and backed up as if I was going to hurt him.

"Stop being elusive, I know something happened to make you go to work for the Scarapino family. Now, tell me what's going on, so we can help you."

"I can't. They'll kill them."

"Who'll kill who?"

'The Scarapinos," he cried out, "They have my wife and son. They are coming here today to get more information on Joey Toranetti."

"I can see your wife must have put up a good fight. Do you know when they are coming?"

"They said six, which is eight hours from now."

"May I use your phone?"

"Yes, of course. It's on the table by the busted television."

Giuseppe called me at the villa and told me about Alissi's wife and son. "How's Alissi taking it? I See. Can I call you back?"

"Yeah. I'll wait for your call."

I gathered everyone around and told them what happened to Alissi's family. "We need to help him. They are coming to his house tonight and want information on my whereabouts. Any suggestions?"

"Joey," Gino said, "why don't we go to his place, stay down the street and when these men get there, we can tail them. They may lead us to his family."

"That's a great idea, Gino. What do you think?"

They all agreed, "That could work."

I called Giuseppe, and told him our plan.

"He needs to have information of your whereabouts tomorrow, Joey."

"Tell him we are going to Naples to see Piazza del Mercato, this market has been there since Roman times, and Castel dell'Ova, it's the oldest castle in Naples."

"If he tells them that, they may ask how he knows."

"He should tell them I told him. They haven't a clue we know he was involved."

"Domenico, listen. We'll help get your wife and son back. You must trust us."

"Why should I trust you?"

"Do you want your family back, unharmed?"

"Yes!"

"Then you have no choice." Giuseppe told Domenico where Joey would be tomorrow. "We will be down the block."

Around 4:30 we left for Officer Alissi's. We arrived near his home and parked down the street. Giuseppe was at our end of the street and stepped into the car. I told everyone, "Don't open the doors, light any cigarettes or do anything that will expose us." Everyone nodded. We waited, and at exactly six o'clock Scarapino's men showed up. They walked into Officer Alissi's home and the next thing I saw was a flash and the sound of gun fire. We drove down to the house, and jumped out of the car just as the men came running out. They saw us and started shooting.

Chapter 6

We opened fire on them and all three went down. The car took off. I walked over to the men and saw one was still alive. He was very young, and I could see his eyes were starting to tear up. "What's your name?" He didn't answer me, just stared up at me with a blank look in his eyes. "Why did you kill him" I asked. Still, he continued to just stare back. "Where is his family?" He continued to stare as a lone tear started to roll down his cheek. He muttered, "I don't want to die"

"I can see that you are only hit in the shoulder, leg, and high in the chest. These aren't critical wounds: you aren't going to die; at least not tonight. What's your name?" I asked again.

"Jimmy"

Are you married?"

"Yes."

"Do you have kids?"

"Yes, two."

"Do you want to see them again?"

"Yes."

"I'll help you, if you'll help me. Where's Alissi's family?"

His tears started to flow, "You'll kill me even if I do tell you."

"I promise I won't. Just tell me where they are" He gave me the address of a warehouse.

"You'd better get there fast; they're going to kill them."

"Giuseppe, do you know where this warehouse is?"

"Yes, it's just a few blocks away."

"Alfredo, check on Alissi, maybe there's some hope. Then call the police and have them send an ambulance for this guy. Let's get to that warehouse." We arrived in five minutes and saw two men entering. I told Janet to get into the driver's seat and wait for us. "Justin watch her." Gino, Giuseppe and I jumped out of the car and raced to the door the two men had just entered. It was still ajar. "Giuseppe, stay here and watch our backs." We walked in, looked around and saw the two men entering a room in the rear of the warehouse. There was a window by the room, I peeked in and saw Alissi's family. The men were taking out their guns. "Now, Gino," I said in a hushed voice. We both crashed through the door at the same time, the men turned to shoot, but we were faster and shot them dead. I walked over to Alissi's wife and asked, "Are you and your son okay?"

"Yes, we're okay. Where's my husband?"

Just then Alfredo walked in and whispered to me, "Alissi is on his way to the hospital, he's in bad shape.."

"Alfredo, take Mrs. Alissi to the hospital, so she can be with her husband. Your father, Janet and I will come with you. Gino, you and Justin take a cab back to the villa."

"I think we should stick together, just in case."

I started thinking about separating and said, "You're probably right. Okay, we'll all go to the hospital. We can keep Mrs. Alissi and her son company."

When we arrived at the hospital I saw Inspector Falcone and a slew of police. Mrs. Alissi came over to me and said, "Thank you. My husband is being operated on, but the doctor said he will live. Because of you my husband is going to be okay."

"I'm happy to hear that." When Inspector Falcone walked over to us I thought we were going to jail.

Chapter 6

"Joey," he said. "Thank you, for saving Domenico's life and rescuing his family. If you need anything, please don't hesitate to ask."

"You're very welcome; I may need to take you up on that." I noticed a nurse coming down the hall and asked "Is the doctor available?"

"How can I help you?"

"I need to find out about the other person that was just brought in"

"He is in the OR. I'll let you know when the doctor comes out."

"Thank you." I turned to Janet and asked, "Would you like something to eat?"

"Yes I'm starving."

"Anyone else want something?" Everyone agreed, including Mrs. Alissi and her son. Inspector Falcone and his men declined.

"I know there is a cafeteria in this hospital, but I saw a little café down the block. I'll come back with enough food for everyone." I turned to Gino, "Do you want to come with me?"

"You bet, I remember the last time we left a hospital to make a food run."

"Ah, yes. You almost died. I don't think that's going to happen again."

"Well, just in case, Joey, let's be ready."

We left the hospital and started walking toward the café when I noticed a car just like the one by Officer Alissi's house. I grabbed Gino and pointed toward the car. The car doors opened and two men in long jackets got out. As we started pulling out our guns, they looked over at us. We started to lift our guns, but the two men walked the other way. Gino and I looked at each other and shuddered. Gino said, "That was a bit hair-raising."

"You can say that again!" We made it to the café bought the food, and went back to the hospital, but didn't mention anything about the car. When I spotted the nurse again I asked, "Can I see the doctor yet?

"He is cleaning up and will see you shortly."

"Thank you, I'll be over there." I pointed to the row of seats where Janet sat.

When the doctor arrived, I walked over and asked. "Can I talk to the man you just worked on?"

"Not yet, he is in recovery."

"How soon can I see him?"

"In about an hour."

"Thank you, I'll wait. While you're here doctor, would you mind if I had someone stay with Domenico at all times?"

"And you are?"

"I'm Joey Toranetti, a friend of the family. I have reason to believe someone might try to finish off Officer Alissi."

"I will call the polizia to keep an eye on him."

"No doctor! We'll handle it. We think someone in the questura is involved."

"I see. Well, as long as you're careful and don't hurt anyone."

"Thank you doctor. We'll be very careful. Maybe, you can put him in a different room without anyone knowing he was moved."

"I can do that."

"Thank you again, doctor. Justin, you will stay by Domenico. No one, but no one, gets near him, except a doctor or a nurse."

Chapter 6

The nurse came over and said, "You can see Jimmy Coronati now Mr. Toranetti."

"Thank you." I went into the recovery room and saw Jimmy with handcuffs hooked to his bed. "Hi Jimmy, I told you that you'd be okay." I smiled at him and he smiled back. "Now, who put you up to kidnapping Alissi's family?"

"I didn't know they were going to kidnap anyone."

"What did you think they were going to do?"

"They told me they were going to teach someone a lesson and they would pay me two hundred dollars. I needed the money, my wife is sick."

"Who's they?"

"I don't know. He called me on the phone." Jimmy cried.

I knew I wouldn't get anywhere. "Okay Jimmy. Get better."

Chapter 7

We stayed a little longer at the hospital then headed back to the villa. As we were driving no one spoke. When we walked in I asked Giuseppe, "Have you heard from Carmine?"

"Not yet, but I'll call him now." When we walked over to the phone Giuseppe noticed there was a message. He pressed the button, and we all listened as Carmine said, *"My family doesn't want a sit-down, they want revenge, they want Joey dead."*

"What now, Joey?" Giuseppe asked.

"Call him back; tell him to keep trying. Just because they said no you can't quit trying."

"I'll call him, but I don't think he'll listen."

Giuseppe dialed Carmine's number as instructed, "Put it on speaker."

Carmine answered the phone and Giuseppe told him not to quit trying. "They won't even listen to me, It's useless. By the way, you should know, my father put out a contract on Joey."

"When did he do that?"

Chapter 7

"Yesterday."

"How much is it for?"

"One hundred thousand dollars." Giuseppe looked at me apprehensively. "Is your father looking for a war? Because that's what's going to happen."

"I'm sorry Giuseppe. They don't care."

"What do you want to do Joey?"

"Carmine, this is Joey. Is that contract public or just one person?"

"Just one person."

"Are you sure?"

"Yes, I'm sure."

"Do you know who?"

"I believe it will be Carlos Tarazini. My father uses him for special assignments."

"Do you know where I can find Carlos?"

"No. Only my father knows."

"Well Carmine, it would be in your best interest if you tell me where I can find your father."

"Why? So, you can kill him?"

"Carmine, I don't want to kill your father, I just want to talk to him."

"I know my father isn't a good person but he's still my father, and I don't believe you won't kill him."

"Let's put it this way, Carmine, I will kill him if he keeps coming after me. So, do yourself a favor and convince him to talk to me." I hung up.

"Giuseppe, do you know where Angelo hangs out?"

"No!"

"I know Carmine said it isn't a public hit, but what do you think?"

"He doesn't like to answer to anyone, so I believe he's just reaching out to a person he trusts."

"Okay. Let's be on the safe side. We'll just have to be more aware of our surroundings from now on. In the meantime, I'll call my father and Augie and have them reach out to the families over here."

"Okay, Joey. Let me know how that goes."

"Giuseppe, are you still with me?" I asked. I'm getting a bad vibe from him. He's not himself, he looks worried. I know we really need him and his connections but I had to give him a way out.

"I really don't want to be, but I never liked the Scarapino family. So, I'm still with you."

I called my father and told him what was happening. He made his thoughts clear, "You need to get out of there and back to Brooklyn."

"I'm sorry Dad, I can't do that. I'll be looking over my shoulder for the rest of my life."

"So, you're going to take on the whole family? That's crazy. Come back here!"

"I'm sorry, Dad, I just can't."

Next, I called Augie and told him what was going on. He told me he would make some calls to the families he knew here and would get back to me.

The tension was running high at the villa. Everyone was feeling the pressure the Scarapino family was causing. I needed to come up with something to alleviate the tension. I looked at

Chapter 7

everyone and stated, "We need to stop being on the defense and start being on the offense."

"How do you expect to do that?" Gino uttered.

"By going to Bari to start."

Giuseppe looked at me and smiled, "That's a great idea Joey. Once we get there, we let people know we are looking for the Scarapinos."

"That's right, Giuseppe. If we ask enough people, the word will get out that we're in Bari."

Janet came over and asked me, "I don't understand Joey. How does that help?"

"It helps because we will be controlling the situation instead of Angelo controlling us."

"What happens if you find out where he is? Are you going after him?"

"No. I'm hoping to force a meeting with him. We should all get a good rest. It's a long drive to Bari."

"Joey," Janet blurted out looking at me sheepishly, "I was looking at the map and want to know if we could stop in Naples on the way?"

"What do you think, Alfredo?"

"It can't hurt. We can stay in Naples tomorrow night and drive to Bari the next morning."

"Okay, Janet. Naples, it is." Janet jumped up and gave me a huge hug, "Thank you, thank you, thank you."

As we were eating dinner Augie called and informed me that the families he knows in Italy were not going to stop us from going after the Scarapinos. "That's great to hear Augie." I told

Augie what we were going to do and he sounded very skeptical, but wished us luck.

"Thank you, Augie. But, why so skeptical?"

"From what I heard about the Scarapinos, Angelo is a lunatic and his wife, Angelina, is as bad a seed as he is, if not worse. They will not sit down with you. And, if they did, it would most likely be a trap."

"So, what do you suggest?"

"Find them and get rid of them. I have heard of this Carlos Tarazini, you'll need to get him, before he gets you. Once he's out of the picture Angelo and his wife will start to worry."

"Do you know where I should look, Augie?"

"No, Joey I haven't a clue. But, there is a cop in Rome that might know."

"What's his name? I'll look him up, give me a minute. I'll never forget him. He tried to pin a murder on me about twenty-five or thirty years ago. His name was Falcone."

"Was he an inspector at that time?"

"No, just an officer. Why?"

"I was arrested by an Inspector Falcone, for killing two men who tried to kill me in my hotel room. It was totally self-defense. Why would he know Carlos?"

"I don't think the person that arrested you could be the same person I knew. He would be around seventy by now. When officer Falcone arrested me, I overheard him telling another officer he was looking for a Carlos Tarazini. From what I remember, he found him in, or near Naples."

"Did he arrest him?"

"No. No proof."

"What about you?"

"He let me go. I had an alibi for the time of the murder."

"I'll go to the station in the morning and confront Inspector Falcone. I hope he knew of this Falcone."

In the morning, I took Gino with me to the station house. On the way, I shared with him what Augie had told me. "So, you think that Inspector Falcone arrested Augie?"

"No, he couldn't have. I know it's a long shot, but maybe he knows him." We arrived at the Questura and I went to the desk and asked to see Inspector Falcone.

"Who are you?"

"I'm Joey Toranetti. Inspector Falcone told me if I needed him, just ask."

The officer picked up the phone, hit a number and waited a few seconds, "Yes, Inspector, there is a Joey Toranetti to see you. Okay. I'll send him back. Down that hall first door on your right."

"Thank you officer."

Gino and I walked over to the Inspector's office and knocked. "Come in." We walked in and the inspector said, "Ciao, Joey, Gino, how can I assist you?" I proceeded to tell him what Augie told me. He replied, "That couldn't be me. I was too young. However, it might have been my father."

"Is there anyway of checking that out, Inspector?"

"I was told my father kept records of everything. Let me check his files. Do you know how long ago this happened?"

"I'm not sure, maybe about twenty-five or thirty years ago."

"Just give me a few minutes, Joey. I have to go to the file room."

"I'm not going anywhere. Take your time."

About thirty minutes later he returned and told us, "I found what you're looking for. It was my father that brought your friend in. His other suspect was a Carlos Tarazini. He had no evidence on either one of them, and had to let them go."

"Is there an address for Tarazini?"

"This was a long time ago, so it may not be a good address, but here it is."

He handed me the address, "It's a place to start. Thank you, Inspector, we'll talk soon." We left and went back to the villa.

Chapter 8

When we arrived at the villa, everyone was ready to go to Naples, including Justin. I looked at him and asked, "When did you get back? And, how is Officer Alissi?"

"I got back about a half hour ago. Officer Alissi is doing well. The family has a friend in northern Italy, by the Swiss border. They will stay with them until it's safe to go back home."

"Who knows where they are?"

"Inspector Falcone. He will let them know when it is safe."

"Great. We're headed to Naples. Are you ready?"

"Yes. We're all ready." Janet replied.

We all piled into Alfredo's car and left. As we were driving I told them of the old address I had for Carlos Tarazini. "Are we just going to kill him?" Gino asked.

"No, Gino. I just want to see if he still lives there."

"And if he does ... then what?"

"I'll figure that out, then. Alfredo, how far is Naples?"

"It will take about two to three hours to get there."

What hotel should we stay at?"

"When we stop, I'll make a call for a reservation. You'll like Hotel Napoli. It was remodeled last year."

We drove for a while then stopped in a small town called Latina. This city is in the Lazio region in central Italy. Janet noticed some great shops along the roadway and wanted to visit them. I figured we had to stop anyway and asked Alfredo if we could pull in there. "This is perfect, Joey. I need to find a rest room and get gas anyway." We pulled into a gas station and Alfredo went to find a rest room and a phone while Giuseppe filled up the tank. Justin and Gino went to a small café to get coffee, while Janet and I did some window shopping. We all needed to walk around a little to stretch our legs.

We came across a beautiful boutique. It turned out to be a clothing and gift shop that Janet adored. We walked in and were amazed at the size of this shop. From the outside, it looked small but on the inside, there were six aisles of women's and men's clothes, and many types of souvenirs. I heard the bell over the entrance door ring. There was a mirror up on the wall by the ceiling. I looked at it out of curiosity and saw two men enter. I didn't think much of it until I heard some yelling coming from the woman behind the counter and the two men. I looked at Janet. As we started to walk toward the front of the store the argument got louder. I heard the woman say, "I am not paying you anything! Now, get out of my store."

One of the men grabbed the woman by her arm and said, "You will pay or we will burn this place down."

Janet and I stood at the front of the aisle and I cleared my throat, "Ahem."

The two men turned and said, in perfect English, "What are you looking at?"

I answered, "At two idiots. Now, let go of the lady and do as she said, get out of her store."

"Mind your business and get outta here."

"I'm only going to say this once more, let go of her!"

Both men pulled out their guns, I pulled my gun out and shot the first man in the chest, the second man shot before I could, but my second shot hit him in the head.

The woman was screaming hysterically, "Your friend is bleeding!"

I looked down and heard Janet crying for me, "Joey! Joey! Help me, I'm bleeding."

I yelled at the woman, "Call an ambulance! Hurry." I put my arms around her shoulders, pulled her up to my chest, hugged and kissed her, and with tears in my eyes I said, "I love you, an ambulance is on its way. You'll be fine." She started to close her eyes, "Don't close your eyes, Talk to me. You're going to be fine, just stay awake." I heard the siren and said, "The ambulance is here, honey. Everything will be fine." She didn't answer me. The paramedics came in, and I said, "She's not answering me."

They pulled me up and knelt down beside her to check and see if she was breathing, "She is still alive, she just passed out. We need to get her to the hospital now!" By this time there were three ambulances at the scene.

Alfredo, Gino, Justin, and Giuseppe heard the sirens and ran toward the sound. That's when they saw me standing by the ambulance. They ran over to me, "What happened Joey?" just as the paramedics were bringing Janet out on one stretcher, a man on another stretcher and a body on yet one more. I was numb. I couldn't think. Gino again asked, "What happened?" The woman from the store told Gino what had happened. Gino looked at me and asked, "How'd this happen, Joey?

"These two guys were trying to shake that woman down. I told them to leave her alone. Instead they pulled out their guns, so I shot the first guy in the chest and when, the second guy fired, I fired back and got him in the head. The second guys shot must've hit Janet."

The women from the store came over to us and said, "I am so sorry about your friend. Why didn't you just leave?"

"She is my wife and my best friend. We have a baby at home." By this time, I was bawling. The tears were coursing down my cheeks and I couldn't restrain my emotions. It took all my strength to get myself under control. "Gino, take me to the hospital."

Gino yelled out to Alfredo, "Let's get to the hospital."

As we were getting into the car an officer came over and said, "You can't leave. You have to come to the Questura and tell us what happened."

I looked him straight in the eye and said, "That's not going to happen. I'm going to the hospital to see my wife. You want a statement, come to the hospital."

"I can't let you do that."

"Try and stop me." I turned toward the car and entered the back seat. We left for the hospital with the polizia following us. They turned on their sirens, not to pull us over, but to escort us. We arrived at the hospital in no time. As we ran in I cried to the nurse, sitting behind the desk, "My wife, Janet Toranetti was just brought in. Where is she?"

"Is she the one that was shot?"

"Yeah! I want to see her."

"She was rushed up to the operating room. She's in bad shape."

"Is she going to be okay?"

"Dr. O'Malley is the best. He will do everything he can to save your wife, Mr. Toranetti."

"Joey." Gino said as he was holding my arm, "Let's sit down and wait for the doctor."

"You're right, Gino." I sat down and didn't say a word for about five minutes, "What about the guy I shot? Is he still alive? I want to talk to him."

"No, he didn't make it."

Just then the officer from the scene of the incident came over and calmly asked if he could get a statement. I told him what had happened. He said, Mr. Toranetti, I'm so sorry for the situation your wife is in. She's in good hands with Dr. O'Malley. He saved my best friend a year ago."

"What happened to your friend?"

"He was shot down by the same type of people that did this today."

"Do you know who these people are?"

"Yes, but no one will come forward to testify against them."

"Are they from around here?"

"No, they are from Bari, but trying to take this area over."

"Would they happen to be the Scarapino family?"

"Yes, how did you know?"

"Just a guess." I then told the officer about our situation.

"What are you going to do?"

"As soon as I know my wife will be okay, I'm going to stop them, for good. "Giuseppe, call Pasquale and get Angelo's address. We're going to pay him a visit."

Giuseppe blurted out, "What are you doing, Joey. I thought the plan was to force Angelo into a meeting!"

"Not anymore. That changed when Janet got shot."

"Joey, you're not thinking straight. This incident was a pure accident. It had nothing to do with the Scarapinos coming after you." I realized that I was being a hothead. My father always told me to stop and think before I made any decisions. Giuseppe continued. "You can't just barge into his home. You'll get yourself and the rest of us killed."

"You're right Giuseppe. I'm not thinking straight, But, I am going to take the Scarapinos down. One way or another, this must end. Now!"

"Now you're thinking." Giuseppe said.

We'll continue to try and force a meeting. But, if that doesn't work, then we'll go after them. Agreed?"

Everyone agreed. "If any of you want out at any time just tell me. There'll be no hard feelings."

No one said a word. Gino walked over and acknowledged, "I'm with you, Joey." A few seconds later, one-by-one, everyone came over and voiced their firm agreement.

"Thank you. Now, please make that call, Giuseppe." While Giuseppe was on the telephone, the doctor walked out of the operating room. I felt myself getting sick to my stomach. I felt like I was going to pass out. As he came closer to me, his face was dismal looking. I started thinking Janet was dead. I felt that the doctor was a long distance away from me, time stopped. I cried out, "How's my wife?"

"She's lost a lot of blood, but she'll be okay. We need to keep an eye on her for a few days."

"When can I see her?"

"You can see her in about an hour. Your wife must stay in the intensive care unit for now. She needs to rest."

"Thank you, Dr. O'Malley."

"I'll have the nurse come and get you as soon as your wife is settled in. I Just want you to know, your wife is one lucky woman, the bullet just missed her spine."

"Thanks again, Doc." I whispered to Gino, "I need to call my father and tell him what happened."

"He's going to have a fit, Joey."

"Yeah, I know. I need to find a phone."

"I saw a phone down the hall. I'll watch for the nurse."

"Thanks, Gino." I called my father's house and my mother answered, "Hi Mom, how's our son doing?"

"Little Joey is doing great. There's something wrong isn't there?"

"Why would you think that?"

"I can hear it in your voice. Is everything okay there?"

"Mom, please put Dad on the phone."

"Now I know something is wrong! Tony, it's Joey." I could hear my mother crying as she said, "Something is very wrong."

My father came to the phone and asked, "What's wrong, Joey?" I told him what happened and he was extremely upset. "As soon as she is feeling better, come home."

"Dad, I need to finish what they started."

"Do you have a death wish, son?"

"No. We're still going to try and set up a meeting. If we can't, then we'll end it our way."

"I don't like this, Joey."

"Neither do I, Dad. But it is what it is."

"What do you want from me?"

"Do you think that you and Rocco can come here and stay with Janet?"

"We'll be there tomorrow afternoon. I just have to say though; I think you're in over your head."

"I have plenty of help Dad. Get a piece of paper and pencil and write down this address." I gave him the address and said, "See you tomorrow." I went back to the waiting room and told Alfredo to get everyone a room. "We won't be leaving until tomorrow afternoon. I'll stay here with Janet."

Gino came over to me and asked, "How did it go with your father?"

"Just as you thought, not very well, he wants us to come home."

"I'm guessing you told him no."

"I'm going to finish what they started, one way or another. Rocco and my father are coming here to stay with Janet. They should be here by tomorrow afternoon."

Alfredo arranged for rooms at a nearby hotel for everyone. The nurse came over to me and informed me, "You can see your wife now Mr. Toranetti. But only for a few minutes."

Chapter 8

"Thank you" I followed her to Janet's room. Rushing in, I gently grabbed and hugged her to my chest as I cried out, "I love you. I thought I lost you."

I love you too. I thought I was dying. All I saw was you and our son drifting away. The next thing, I'm in this room."

"The doctor said you'll be fine. You'll have to stay a few days to rest up. You lost a lot of blood. Try and get some rest."

"Are you leaving?"

"No, I'll be right here with you until you fall asleep. Now close your eyes and get some rest."

When Janet fell asleep, I walked out to the waiting room and asked Giuseppe, "Did Pasquale give you the address?"

"He doesn't have an address, but he'll take us there."

"Is he coming here?

"He will be here in the morning. I gave him the hotel's address and your room number."

"Okay. But, before we leave we need to find Tarazini."

Chapter 9

The next morning I was up early. I started making coffee and was trying to be quiet, when Gino came out, "Good morning Joey. Why are you up so early?"

"Hi Gino, I hope I didn't wake you?"

"No, you didn't. I smelled the coffee."

"I just couldn't sleep. I'm worried about Janet."

"She's going to be okay. She just needs to rest."

"I know; I'm really worried. I'm also infuriated that I still don't know who it is that told the Scarapinos we were coming to Italy."

"Doesn't your father know yet?"

"He would have told me if he knew. I guess I should've asked when I called him. The coffee is ready, would you like some? It smells strong."

"Yeah, I'll just add some water."

Around 6:30 there was a knock on the door, I looked through the peep hole and saw Pasquale. He and his body guard came in and I asked if they wanted coffee. They both replied, "No thank you. There is a café down the block. Let's go there." Pasquale offered "Where's your wife?" I told him what happened and that the men I killed, were from the Scarapino family. "How do you know?"

"The police told me."

"This is news to me, I didn't know Angelo was trying to expand."

I looked at them and blurted, "This coffee is horrible. Gino, get everyone up and let's go to the café down the street." The café was only a block away so we walked. When we arrived I requested a table for seven.

After we all placed our orders I turned to Pasquale, "Where is Angelo located?"

"He's on the outskirts of Bari. He purchased a large villa there."

"Before we go there we need to find Carlos Tarazini."

"Why, Joey?"

I told him about the contract the Scarapino family put out on me, "Carmine informed us that Tarazini would be the hitter."

"I know Carlos, he wouldn't accept the contract."

"Why."

"He retired a year ago, he's seventy years old!"

"Then why did Carmine tell us that?"

"Carmine knows nothing about that part of his father's business."

"Do you think he made this a public hit?"

"I don't think there's a contract. Knowing Angelina I would bet she wants to kill you herself."

"Do you have a way to confirm that?"

"I'll call Carlos and ask him."

"Call him from the hotel. I have to get to the hospital."

We all finished eating and walked back to the hotel. I asked Alfredo to take me to the hospital and reminded Pasquale to call Carlos.

Pasquale called Carlos and asked him about the contract, "So, there is no contract. Thanks, Carlos."

When I entered the hospital, I walked over to the information desk and asked, "Am I too early to see my wife in the ICU?"

"What's your wife's name?" I told her, she looked at her notes and informed me, "Your wife has been moved to a regular room. Room number 128."

"That's great. How do I get there?"

"Just follow this corridor around to the elevators and make a right. Then go to room 128."

"Thank you." When I stepped into the room I saw Janet sitting up eating breakfast. "How are you doing, honey? You look a whole lot better."

"I'm feeling a little better. Doctor O'Malley told me I was doing better than he expected. He said I would be released in a day or two."

"That's fantastic news. I called my father and told him what happened and he told us to come home."

"How is little Joey?"

"He is doing well."

"What did you say about coming home?"

"I told him no. Instead, I asked him and Rocco to come here and stay with you."

"Are they coming?"

They'll be here this afternoon."

"Then what? I suppose you're still going after the Scarapinos."

"Yeah, I am! This has to end!"

"Don't I have a say in this? The only thing I see ending is you getting killed."

"Look, I still want to see if we can meet to end this without any more bloodshed."

Just then the nurse came in to check Janet's vitals. Janet looked at me, "This conversation isn't over Joey!"

I know she's mad, but I have to do what I feel is right. "I know honey. Now, try and get some rest before my father and Rocco get here. I'm going to get some coffee. Can I get you something?'

"No, thank you." She said sarcastically.

I went down to the cafeteria and as I passed the entrance to the hospital I saw Gino and Justin walking in, "Hey Gino, Justin, what's going on?"

"We wanted to see how Janet was doing."

"She's doing great, just mad at me."

As we were walking to the cafeteria, I told them how sarcastic she sounded and Gino looked at me and offered, "She's just scared, Joey. She doesn't want anything happening to you."

"I know, but I have to take care of this situation. I'm not going to live my life as a mark and endanger my family. She's just going to have to accept that. Let's go to her room. My father and brother should be here soon."

We walked back to Janet's room. As we approached we heard voices. It was my father and Rocco. "Dad … Rocco … when did you get here?" I was ecstatic to see them. It made me feel like I was home.

"We arrived a few minutes ago. How are you, Joey?"

"I'm fine. How was your trip?"

"It was long, but uneventful." My father turned to Gino and Justin and asked, "How are you two holding up."

"We're doing good, considering all that's happening."

"I understand. Janet looks great, considering she was shot." Then my father looked directly at me with a scowl on his face.

"Yeah, she's a fast healer." I interjected with a smile and a quick wink at Janet. "Dad, have you found out who the rat is that told the Scarapinos we were coming here?"

"Well, kind of."

"I don't understand."

"Augie found out who he was. Do you know Alberto Perini?"

"I've heard the name before. I don't think I met him though. Have you talked to him?"

"No, we can't find him."

"Have you asked Augie?"

"All Augie said was, he left town and won't be back."

"Oh, I understand."

"Joey, you need to come home now. Forget about the Scarapinos."

"Dad, let's not start that again. You know I have to finish what they started. If I walk away now, I'll always be a marked man." My father looked at me and nodded his understanding.

"Janet," my father stated, "You can come back with us."

"No!" Janet replied, "I'm staying here with Joey."

"Are you nuts? Go back to New York with them! I want you safe."

"I told you before; I'm not going without you. And that's final."

"Joey," my father said, "What's your intention? Do you want to kill the Scarapinos or make peace with them?"

"What I want is to exterminate them, but that would make me just like them. So, I guess, if at all possible, I'll have to settle for making peace with them."

Just then Giuseppe and Pasquale opened the door and poking their heads in asked. "Joey, may we talk to you?"

My father saw them and asked, "Who are they Joey?"

"Dad, this is Giuseppe Caladessi, he is Alfredo's father and the leader of the Caladessi Family in Rome. The other guy is Pasquale, Augie's friend. He's the one who called Augie."

"I see. It's a pleasure to meet you." They entered and the three shook hands.

"What do you want to talk about?"

"We overheard what you said to your father. Forget about making peace."

"Why?"

"We just saw Carmine outside the hospital getting out of a cab. He told us his father is sending men here to kill you and your wife."

"How does he know we're here?"

"Remember, the two men you killed? He heard your wife was shot and in the hospital."

"Does he know when they're coming?"

"No, but he said we'd better leave, and fast!"

I went to the closet, removed Janet's clothes, and told her, "Get dressed, we have to leave." Janet took her clothes and went into the bathroom to dress. When she came out she exclaimed, "I'm supposed to be resting."

"You can rest in the car. Gino, Justin, make sure no one is coming. Dad, Rocco, help Janet to the car. Alfredo, give the nurse my insurance card, tell her to send the paperwork to your home. We'll meet you at the car. Now, let's go." I split everyone up into two cars, Giuseppe, Pasquale, Rico, Justin and Carmine went in Pasquale's car. Janet, my father, Rocco, Gino, and I were in Alfredo's. Alfredo came out, got into the driver's seat, and started the car. As we were getting into the cars I noticed two cars pull up to the front doors of the hospital, three men from each car stepped out and started walking toward the front doors. I saw one of the men peer into Pasquale's car. He must have recognized Carmine. He tapped one of the other men and pointed toward Carmine, yelling, "That's them!"

Chapter 9

I immediately said to Alfredo, "Let's get outta here!" With the screeching of our tires we took off, Pasquale was right behind us. The men started shooting at us. I yelled out, "Get on the floor!" Pointing at my father, Rocco and Janet I added. "And hold on!" Alfredo turned left at the next corner on two wheels, Pasquale was right behind us. The men had swiftly rushed back to their cars and the chase was on. Alfredo headed toward a main road and we must have been going seventy miles an hour. Rico, who was driving Pasquale's car, pulled up alongside of us motioning to split up. At the very next street Alfredo made a right, again on two wheels, and I saw Rico go left. The men in the first car followed Rico; the others stayed with us and started shooting.

Alfredo looked at us and said, "Hold on everyone, I'm going to spin around." Alfredo made a quick U-turn and stopped. We were now facing the other car. They jammed on their brakes. They started to get out of the car, but weren't fast enough. Alfredo, Gino, and I jumped out of the car and opened fire.

They never knew what happened. We walked over to their car and saw they were all dead. Peering into our car I asked, "You guys okay?" They answered they were all fine. I yelled out to Alfredo, "We need to find Rico"

We drove back to where Rico had made the left. That's when we saw the other car turning into an alley, and we heard the shooting. We pulled into the alley and saw Rico shooting at the men. I watched as Rico went down, Pasquale ran towards him, shooting at the men. So, we opened fire on the men from behind, and they all went down. Walking over to Pasquale I asked, "How's Rico?"

"He's okay, got hit in the arm, the bullet went clean through."

"Great. Now let's get outta here before the cops get here."

"Alfredo," Pasquale said, "Where do you want to meet back up?"

"Hotel Napoli, do you know it?"

"Yeah, we'll see you there."

Chapter 10

We arrived at the Hotel Napoli and waited for Pasquale. While we waited, Alfredo told me he knew the owner and went inside to get rooms for the night. When Alfredo came out he had a real big man with him. He was at least six feet five inches tall with muscles on top of muscles. He might just be the biggest man I had ever seen. His hair was jet black, his eyes were a steely gray. I would never want to run into him in a dark alley. When they approached, Alfredo said, with a broad smile, "Joey, this is my friend Alessandro."

"It's a pleasure meeting you." When we shook hands, I was hoping he didn't crush mine. Surprisingly enough his handshake was very gentle.

"Alfredo speaks highly of you Mr. Toranetti."

"Please, call me Joey."

"Okay, Joey. I'll tell you this, as long as you're here, no one, and I mean no one, will bother you or your party." I guess I had a puzzled look on my face because Alessandro explained.

"Alfredo told me what happened, see those two men over there," I looked at where he pointed and saw two men, just as big as Alessandro, playing cards. "They will be watching your back while you're here."

"Thank you very much, Alessandro. Were you able to get us rooms?"

"I only have three rooms available, but they each have two bedrooms and a pull-out sofa. I hope that isn't an inconvenience?"

"Not at all, we'll work it out." We reserved all three rooms just as Pasquale pulled up. I walked over to Carmine and said, "Thank you for warning us about your father's men."

"I don't understand my father's thinking, but I couldn't stop him. I knew I had to do something."

"We appreciate what you did. How are you feeling?"

"Not very well. I thought I was going to die in that alley."

"That's why I'm asking this. I need to know how many men are with your father at his villa."

"Why, are you going to take him out after all?"

"I warned you, Carmine, if your father continues to come after me I will stop him, one way or another. It is one thing to threaten me, but my wife? He's crossed the line."

"After what happened today, I have no doubt that you won't hesitate to off him. Please let me talk to him again."

"It's too late. I can't trust him."

"Please, Joey, let me just try one more time."

"I will think about it and let you know. Let's all get some lunch."

Chapter 10

Before we went into the restaurant I pulled my father aside and told him about Carmine and he replied, "Are you nuts? You can't trust his father."

"I know, Dad. That's exactly what I told him."

"Well, do what you think is best, Joey, but be careful. Oh, I need a gun."

"Why, Dad, we'll handle everything, you're still sick."

"Yeah, I'm sick, but not dead. I'll feel better if I had a little insurance, shall we say."

"Alfredo, if you still have the spare, would you give it to my father?"

"Yeah, sure. I'll get it for you."

After lunch, I took Carmine aside and stated in no uncertain terms, "We are going to be here tonight and tomorrow night, so, you have until then to talk to your father. Before we go any further, I need to know how many men stay at his villa?"

"There are a total of ten men, not counting my mother and father."

"Remember this, Carmine, anything goes wrong, I won't hesitate to take them out."

"I know, Joey."

"Were going to our room so Janet can rest, I suggest you do the same and think about how you can get you father to listen. This is his last chance to avoid an all-out war."

Carmine called his father as soon as he entered his room. The phone rang a few times before his mother, Angelina, answered,

"Hi, Mom. Is Dad around?"

"What is it, Carmine?"

"I need to speak to Dad, Mom."

"Whatever you want to tell him, you can tell me, dear."

Carmine heard his father yell in the background, "Give me the phone, Angie. What is it Carmine?"

"Your men tried to kill me today."

"They were there to get Joey and his wife. They were doing their job!"

"So, I become disposable? I'm your son!"

"I'm sorry Carmine, they weren't told to hurt you."

"Well, they tried to kill me. Joey and his people saved me. All your men are dead, and Joey is coming for you."

"Let him come. I'll destroy him and his friends."

"You're a fool, Dad. These guys will destroy you. I can still set up a meeting for the two of you. This way nobody else dies."

"Give me your number and I'll call you back."

"No, Dad, I'll call you, in one hour."

"What's the matter, Carmine? You don't trust me?"

"No, Dad, I don't. One hour, have an answer for me."

Giuseppe, who was in the room asked Carmine, "What did your father say?"

"He will think about having a meeting."

I see, I hope he makes the right decision for your sake, Carmine."

Chapter 10

"I hope so too." In exactly one hour Carmine called his father back and asked, "Are you going to meet with Joey?"

Well, you mother is against it, she wants Joey dead, but I'll meet with him. Bring him here to the villa, and we'll talk."

"No tricks, Dad!"

"I give you my word, no tricks. Maybe we can work this out." When Carmine got off the phone he thought, He's up to something, it's always been, whatever my mother wants she gets. My father is up to something.

The next morning Carmine came to my room and told me about the meeting. I looked at Carmine and said, "I have to discuss this with everyone first before I give you my answer. We will talk about it during breakfast."

"Okay, Joey. Can I be present?"

"Of course, you can." I called the front desk and asked the woman, "Do you have a conference room?"

"Yes, we do, Mr. Toranetti. When do you need it?"

"We need it this morning and would like to have breakfast brought in."

"I'll check the schedule, please hold." She picked up the phone again, "We can have the room and a waiter at ten o'clock for you, Mr. Toranetti."

"That's great. Thank you." I looked over at Carmine and said, "Tell everyone, in your room, to come to the conference room, just off the lobby, before ten o'clock."

When we arrived at the conference room Alessandro was there to greet us. "Good morning everyone." He introduced us to our server, "This is Riccardo, your server. He likes to be called Rickey. He will get you whatever you need. We have taken it upon ourselves to set up a table, in the front of the room, with coffee, espresso, tea and sweets. So, please help yourselves."

"Thank you, Alessandro, it's really appreciated." We helped ourselves to the coffee and Danish, gave our orders to Rickey and sat at the table. Everyone was talking about the things that had happened in the last few days. I could tell they were getting edgy. When we finished breakfast, I told them about the meeting Carmine set up with his father. Everyone knew of the meeting. I was the first to say, "I, personally, do not trust Angelo, nor do I like the fact, it is at his villa."

My father stated, "Going to his villa is like going into the lion's den. It's not wise."

Well, Dad, what do you suggest?"

"You need to meet in a neutral place, like a crowded restaurant."

"I agree with you, Dad, except for one thing. The crowds won't bother these people, they don't care who gets caught in the cross-fire."

"I have an idea," Alfredo offered, I know a restaurant, across the street from the Questura. I don't think they will attack us there."

Carmine jumped in, "The cops are on my father's payroll so they won't interfere."

Chapter 10

I think Alfredo's idea will work," Pasquale interjected, "Not all the cops are on the take, only the higher ups and a few followers."

"I like it," I told Alfredo, "That's the best idea so far. Anyone else have a better idea?" No one answered. "Carmine, get with Alfredo for the address and call your father. Tell him we won't meet at his villa, instead we'll meet him at the restaurant."

"What if he says no?"

"Tell him he has no choice. Meet at the restaurant or we'll come to the villa, but not for a meeting." I looked over to Janet and revealed, "Today, we're going to visit Naples."

"Really?" Janet cried out, "Even with all this going on?"

"Yes, I promised you we would see Naples, and that is where we're going. We leave within the hour."

Rocco came over to me and whispered, "Give me a gun."

"No, Rocco, you won't need one. When we go to the restaurant Justin and Dad will stay with you and Janet."

"I want to help you Joey."

"You can help by staying with Dad and Janet. Dad and Justin both have guns to protect you."

"I'm not a baby anymore Joey. I'm not afraid."

"I didn't think you were, Rocco. It's just that you've never had to kill anyone before. It's not as easy as you think, and besides you really never get over it. So, do yourself a favor and just stay with Janet."

"Okay, Joey, you're right."

There were only six of us that went to Naples, Alfredo, Janet, My father, Rocco, Gino and I. The rest of our group went on ahead to Bari. They wanted to check out the layout and the area surrounding it. Before they left I told Carmine to call me at the hotel about the meeting. "I will call you tonight, Joey."

"Okay. Don't forget it's the restaurant or nothing."

As we entered Naples we noticed how colorful and chaotic everything seemed. The population seemed to spill out into the streets all the way down to the harbor. As we were walking toward the harbor we heard many people singing like they were opera stars.

Alfredo said to us, "All these people think they are stars and are waiting to be discovered."

"The way they sound, I would bet some of them are." Janet exclaimed.

When we arrived at the Naples Harbor, Alfredo read from a brochure. This harbor is the gateway to the Mediterranean and the world. Naples harbor is divided into separate docks and basins by a series of piers and breakwaters. Extending east from the Piazza del Municipio is the Molo Angioino,(the pier of the great Angeovin , King Henry the II) with the Marine Station. To the west of this is the Eliporto (Heliport), from which there are regular helicopter services to Capri, Ischia, and Capodichino Airport. Naples is the principal port of Southern Italy."

We decided to have an early dinner along the harbor. The café had tables right next to the water. We were told that Naples made the first pizza and it was the very best. We had to try it and ordered two Margarita Pizzas. I must say it was the best I ever had. After we ate we headed back to our hotel. When we arrived

Chapter 10

Janet wanted to lie down, she was exhausted from all the walking. My father was just as tired so he went with her. The rest of us went to the bar in the hotel. After a few drinks we retired to our respective rooms for the night.

Chapter 11

The next morning my phone rang, "Hello? Oh hi, Justin. Did you check out the area?"

"Yeah. There are a few streets Angelo's men can attack from."

"Draw a diagram of the streets and check out the restaurant."

"We checked the restaurant last night. It's a good size place."

"Can you make a diagram of it too?"

"I can. I will have everything you need when you arrive. There isn't a private room and don't sit near any windows."

"What is the name of the restaurant?"

"The name is Casa de Arturo. Can you give me an idea of when you'll arrive?"

"I'm still waiting for Carmine to call me. Is he with you?"

"No, he's at his father's house trying to convince him to accept the meeting change."

"Have him call me as soon as possible. We'll be there around six o'clock. Don't tell anyone!'

"I won't. See you tomorrow night."

Chapter 11

"Give me a number where I can reach you."

I wrote down the number just as Janet came out of our room and asked, "Who was that, Joey?"

"Justin, he's making a diagram of the area and the restaurant."

"And? What did he say?" I told her everything he said and she just stared at me. Her expression told me she was worried.

"Please don't worry, honey. Everything will be okay." When everyone was up we went to breakfast and I told them what Justin had observed near the restaurant. I asked Alfredo, "How long of a drive is it to Bari?"

"From here it's about two hours. There's a shortcut, but I don't know it."

"Providing Angelo agrees to the meeting, we'll leave here at one this afternoon. I want to be in Bari early."

"Have you heard from Carmine yet?" My father wondered.

"Not yet, but he'll be calling soon." Twenty minutes later Carmine called, "Hi Carmine, So, what's the verdict?"

"My father will meet you at the restaurant at ten tomorrow morning. He said he'll meet with you and only you."

"Anything else?"

"Yeah; no heat or body guards."

"Okay. That's not a problem. He'd better do the same"

"He will. I'll make sure of it."

"Okay, Carmine. Tell your father I'll see him in the morning." I looked at Janet and said, "I want you, my father and Rocco to stay here."

"No way, Joey. Your father and Rocco can stay here, but I'm coming with you."

"Janet, stop being so stubborn! This could get very dangerous and I almost lost you once already. Isn't that enough?"

"I know how to use a gun and; I can handle myself. So, I'm coming with you."

My father looked at me and stated flatly, "We're all coming with you, Joey, and that's final."

I stood there, shook my head. *I have enough on my mind, fighting with them isn't going to work.* "Be ready at one." Just before we left I called Justin and asked, "Have you made all the diagrams?"

"Yeah. I have all the streets in the area mapped out. I have all entrances and exits in the restaurant marked and even where you should and shouldn't sit."

"Great. We'll meet at your hotel and leave here in thirty minutes, I only need the address." I jotted down the address and their room numbers. Then I leaned over and whispered to Alfredo, "Can you get a few suppressors?" I figured we may need silencers.

"I have a friend in Bari that may be able to get a few" Alfredo called his friend and was told we could get six suppressors."

"That's great. We may need them."

Before we left I went down to the manager's office to thank Alessandro for his hospitality and he told me, "If you need me please call. I have many connections in Bari."

"Thank you, I'll do that."

We arrived in Bari around five-thirty and went straight to the hotel. Alfredo made the arrangements. It was small. More like a motel really, except all the rooms were inside. The place was very clean and offered valet service. They had to have this service because of limited parking in the area. I walked into the diminutive lobby and noticed a few cocktail tables with chairs and, a coffee station by the rear wall. Several people sat chatting their afternoon away. I also observed the people sitting around, stopped talking, and were staring at us. I stared back, smiled, and offered a, "Buona sera." They smiled back and said the same to me. When I reached the front desk, I asked the young lady, behind the desk, "May I have two rooms?"

"How many nights, sir?"

"Just one night."

I filled out a registration card and handed it back to her. She noticed the people staring at me and said, "Please don't mind these people. You're a stranger and they are very nosey."

I smiled and assured her, "It's okay. We get that a lot since we came to Italy." I paid cash and said, "If we leave early, where do we drop off the keys?"

"There is a slot in the door, just drop them in there."

"Thank you."

Here are your keys. Your rooms are on the first floor."

"Thank you, very much." I looked at the room numbers and noticed they were near Justin's rooms. *Is this a coincidence or a setup?* I started to walk away and turned to the young lady and asked. "Is there a nice restaurant around here?"

"Yes, about a mile down this road, on your left. It's called Vincenzo's."

"Thank you." We went to our rooms, unpacked and I went to Justin's room, I knocked on his door and called out, "Hi Justin, we're here." Entering I said, "I was told of a good restaurant down the road."

"Vincenzo's."

"Yeah, why? Have you been there?"

"Yeah, it's the only place around here. I think the lady at the front desk gets a commission for sending people there. And, besides, Pasquale and Rico know the owner."

"Is the food good?"

"Yeah. It's really pretty good."

I called the restaurant and asked if they had a table for ten and they did. The person on the other end continued, "What time should we expect you?"

"Can we come in now?"

"Sure, what's the name?"

"Joey. We'll be there in ten minutes."

"I will have your table ready."

When we arrived at the restaurant I noticed a few cars in the parking lot. The building was all red brick. Over the entrance to the restaurant was a sign in blue neon lights spelling Vincenzo's. A beautiful garden with various colored plants and flowers decorating the left and right sides of the entrance greet arriving diners. Spotlights shined on the shrubbery, bringing out various hues of the bushes. A pathway made of elegant slate tiles, led to the front entrance which had stunning, dark oak doors.

When we walked in, I observed a highly varnished matching dark Oak bar on the right side of the room. In front of the bar

Chapter 11

were eight matching bar stools. Four customers sat at the bar deep in conversation. The pleasant looking, woman bartender, offered us a huge pleasant smile. Ten tables of four stood in the middle of the room with white tablecloths and black napkins. Three of the tables were full. On the left side of the room I saw five tables put together and set up the same way. A hostess came over and asked, "Are you Joey, our party of ten?"

"Yes, we are."

"We have your tables ready, sir."

As we followed the hostess to our tables I said, "I spoke to a gentleman when I made the reservation, was he the owner?"

"Yes, that was my husband, Vincenzo."

"Well, you certainly have a beautiful place."

"Thank you. He will be your server."

While we were waiting, I couldn't help noticing that two men at the bar kept looking over at us. I looked at Pasquale and asked. "Do you know the men at the bar?"

He looked at them and replied, "No, I don't. Rico, do you know those men?"

Rico didn't even look and said, I saw them when we came in, they are body guards for some people I know."

"For the Scarapinos?"

"No. I would have told you if they were."

"Then, who Rico?"

"They protect two corporate executives. They were robbed a few times. They are here with the people at the table near the rear of the restaurant."

"Do they know Angelo." When I asked, I must have had a worried look on my face.

"Don't worry Joey," Pasquale offered. "No one would dare mess with anyone at Vincenzo's restaurant."

"Why's that Pasquale?"

Just then Vincenzo came over, "Hi Pasquale, Rico. How are you tonight?"

"We are fine Vincenzo. I'd like you to meet my friend Joey Toranetti."

"It's a pleasure meeting you, Joey"

We shook hands and I replied, "It's great meeting you also." I introduced everyone else to him.

After Vincenzo took our orders and left, I turned to Pasquale and asked, "Why is it that no one will mess with Vincenzo?"

"Because he was the personal chef for one of the biggest families in Calabria, Vito Pantone. This is one of the families that Augie called on your behalf. Vito told Augie he can't interfere because of a pact he has with Angelo. He also told Augie that he would do nothing to stop you from handling this matter."

I looked at Pasquale and stated, "That's what I was told by Augie, now it's confirmed."

My father turned to me and replied, "Good, we won't have any interference."

Our drinks and food came. At the end of our meal we discussed our plan of action. Vincenzo came over and asked, "How was everything?"

"The food was fantastic."

"Good! Now, listen to me. Do not trust Angelo, at this meeting, and watch out for his wife. I guarantee she will be there someplace."

"How do you know about the meeting?"

"Joey, everyone in Bari knows about this meeting. Just be careful."

"I don't trust him, Vincenzo. Do you know the owner at that restaurant?"

"Yes, why?"

"Can he be trusted?"

"Yes, he hates Angelo and his wife. Why? What are you thinking?"

"I would like to put two men in there as workers."

"I can set that up for you. Who do you want in there?"

"I want Gino and Justin to work as prep cooks. Justin told me they open for lunch and start prepping at seven in the morning."

"I will call Arturo tonight. Have your men there at seven."

Thank you, Vincenzo, I owe you."

I told Gino and Justin the plan and told them what to bring and gave them two of the suppressors. I turned to Alfredo, "You, my father, Janet and I will drop Gino and Justin off at six-forty-five. Once they're inside, we will park in an area where we can see the entire front of the restaurant. Pasquale, Rico, and Giuseppe, you will park in an area to watch the rear of the restaurant." I gave two suppressors to Pasquale and Rico in the second car. Alfredo, Janet my Father, Rocco, and I were in our car, I told them, "I know, in my gut, this is a trap so if you need to shoot anyone outside the restaurant use these. I don't want Angelo to hear any gunshots. But don't shoot anyone unless you absolutely have to."

Chapter 12

When Gino and Justin arrived at the rear of the restaurant they opened the door and walked in. A man, wearing the name tag, Roberto, approached and showed them where their stations were. Gino looked around as he navigated the room. The prep station had two six-foot stainless steel tables adjoined together in the middle of the kitchen. On the back wall were the cooking stations, and on the front wall were two more six foot tables placed side-by-side. These tables had warming lights hanging above them; this was where the servers picked up their orders.

To the right were the swinging doors into the restaurant. One marked exit and the other marked entrance. To the right of those doors was yet another six-foot table for putting trays down and next to that table were open storage cabinets on wheels that held all types of cooking implements. To the left rear was a door that led to a storage room.

Chapter 12

About an hour before the meeting a car pulled up to the rear of the restaurant, two men and a woman got out and went through the back door, which led into the kitchen where Gino and Justin where. Pasquale said, "Neither of those men are Angelo. The woman, I believe is Angelo's wife. I didn't get a good look at her. Carmine, is that your mother?"

"Yes, I told you she wants to kill Joey herself."

"I know, but, you didn't tell me she would be here, Carmine. Are you setting Joey up?"

"No, I swear, I didn't know."

Pasquale said to Rico, "Go inside and warn Joey."

Angelina is married to Angelo and is a cold-hearted, psychotic killer who hates Joey, for killing her godson. She will kill anyone who gets in her way.

The two men passed by Justin and stopped by the swinging doors into the restaurant and watched Angelina head towards the ladies' restroom.

Rico walked through the back door, saw Justin, went over to him and whispered, "That woman's Angelina."

One of the men recognized Rico and pulled his gun. Justin quickly drew his silencer enhanced piece and shot him. Gino eliminated the other man.

In the meantime, Justin looked at Gino and whispered, "The woman is Angelina, it's a trap. We need to warn Joey."

"I had a feeling it was. I can't do it now; Angelo is coming in and walking toward a table by a window. If I go out there now it'll spook him."

Justin peered out the doors, saw where Angelo was going to sit and said, "I hope Joey remembers what I told him."

"He will, Justin. He never forgets anything."

I walked into the restaurant at ten o'clock, looked around and saw a man, whom I presumed was Angelo, sitting at a table by a window, I remembered what Justin had said, *Stay away from the windows.*

"You must be Angelo?"

"Yes, I am. Come and sit down."

I looked around and picked a table that had a full view of all the entrances into the dining room and away from a window. "Let's sit here."

"Why? What's wrong with this table, Joey?"

"I don't sit with my back to windows or doors. It's an old habit."

"Okay, I'll sit wherever you'd like." He walked over, sat facing me and stated, "Not trusting me is not a good start for our talks, Joey."

"You can't blame me, Angelo. You've tried to kill me more than once."

"Yes, that's true, I'll give you that. Now, why this meeting?"

"I'm a firm believer in talking things over with my adversaries before going off the deep end. So, why do you want to kill me Angelo?"

"Because you killed my godson."

"We both know it was in self-defense, so cut the crap. That's not the reason, and you know it."

"Please, tell me what you think."

"First, tell your wife to come out, unarmed, or she's dead!"

"What makes you think she is here?"

"I knew this was a trap, especially when my friends came out of the kitchen.

"I don't know what you're talking about."

Gino yelled out, "Your wife is in the ladies room, your two men are dead. Now, tell her to come out."

Angelo paused, looked around, then at Gino. "Now, Angelo!"

Gino and Justin walked toward Joey. Angelo was now able to see them clearly. He looked at me seemingly shocked. After a few seconds, he called out, "Angie come out, unarmed or they will kill you."

Angelina came out, unarmed, looked around in amazement, saw Justin and Gino, and walked over to her husband, as I offered, "Please join us Angie. We were about to discuss our terms."

"What terms?" Angie asked raising one well-shaped eyebrow.

"We're going to come to terms where you stop trying to off me. I killed your godson because he tried to kill me. It was self-defense."

Angie replied, "He was still my godson. You will pay for that!"

Angelo said to his wife, "Shut up Angie, you're only making matters worse." Angie looked at her husband her eyes brimming with rage. "The two men you brought with you are dead. Now, we must talk with Mr. Toranetti and at least consider his terms."

A car pulled up to the restaurant and four men, including the driver, exited the car with rifles and pistols. They entered the restaurant. Alfredo saw the men and quickly drove to the restaurant and yelled out, "Here we go!"

"Gino saw the men coming in and yelled, "Joey, get down!"

As I dove to the floor, I saw Angelo and his wife run toward the bathrooms, the men started shooting their automatic weapons, Gino and Justin were shooting back, Gino slid a gun over to me, I grabbed the gun and shot one of the men. Alfredo and my father came bursting in and the shooters were caught in a crossfire.

Pasquale, Rico, and Giuseppe came running in from the rear, by the time they came in, two of the shooters were dead. I saw my father shoot one of the men. The last man was coming toward me, I raised my gun, pulled the trigger, nothing happened All I heard was a click. The man fired as I rolled under the table, thankfully he missed. I heard a shot and then a thud. When I looked out from under the table I saw Janet. She was standing there, holding a gun, and shaking. I ran over to her, took the gun out of her hand, wrapped my arms around her and said, "It's okay honey, you're going to be okay."

Behind me I caught the sound of my brother's voice, "Janet, are you okay?"

I turned to him and replied, "She'll be okay, Rocco. She just needs some time."

She started crying uncontrollably, then said, "I had to shoot him, he was trying to kill you."

"I know, I know. It's over now. Everything is going to be okay. Where'd you get the gun, honey?"

"Off the floor."

I figured it was one of the dead men's.

My father and brother came over to console Janet. I looked around but didn't spot Angelo or his wife. "Look for Angelo and his wife?" I yelled out as I was consoling Janet.

Gino and everyone searched the restaurant, Gino cried out, "There's a back door here, someone must have picked them up."

I looked over at Pasquale, Bring Carmine here."

"Okay." When Pasquale got to his car, Carmine was gone. "Damnit, he's gone!"

Pasquale came back in the restaurant, told me about Carmine, I said, "It must have been Carmine that picked them up. We've been set up. Let's get outta here before the police get here." I told everyone to go back to Alessandro's hotel in Naples. As we got in our cars I wasn't surprised when I didn't see anyone coming out of the Questura. Pasquale told us to follow him, he knew a shortcut. It took us less than two hours to get back to the hotel.

Chapter 13

When we arrived at the hotel; Alessandro came over to me and asked, "Is everyone okay?

"Everyone but my wife."

"What happened, does she need medical help?"

"She killed a man trying to save me. She's not doing well."

"I have a friend that's a psychologist. I'll have him come over and talk with her."

That would be great. Thank you." Alessandro gave us the same three rooms we had occupied before. My father and brother walked Janet to our bedroom and put her on the bed. I walked in and asked her, "How are you doing?"

"I'll be okay."

"Okay." I walked out of the room and went over to my father, "Dad, I want you to go back to Brooklyn, and take Janet with you."

"Aren't you coming?"

Chapter 13

"No, I'm going to finish this." I walked over to Gino and asked him to get everyone together. I need to talk to them. Gino left and about five minutes later everyone came in. "Listen up; I want to thank every one of you for what you've done for me today. I can't tell you how much I appreciate it. However, I am going to Angelo's villa and finishing this tomorrow night. I understand if you don't want to go."

Gino yelled out, "I'm coming with you!" Then, as before, every-one agreed with a simple nod.

Justin asked, "Do you have a plan or are we just going to bust in on them?"

"I'll have a plan as soon as Pasquale sits down with me. I'll let you in on it after I talk to him." Just about then Janet came out of our room and I asked, "Feeling better honey?"

"Yes, but I need to talk to you."

"I'll be right there. I'll talk to you guys later." Once we were in our room Janet shot me a look of exasperation.

"What's wrong, honey?"

"Don't honey me, Joey Toranetti. I'm not going back without you.

Janet, it's not safe for you to stay here. Especially now. You're not in any shape to deal with what has to be done."

"I need to be here with you."

"Okay, but you'll stay here with my father and Rocco. If not, you're going back to Brooklyn with them. Do you understand?"

"Janet just stared at me but finally agreed. I'll stay here and wait for you. You had better come back or I'll kill you myself." She started to laugh as she thought about what she said, and I laughed with her.

I looked at her and said, "Once this is over we'll go back to Brooklyn and take a real vacation."

"Please be careful, Joey. And come up with a good plan."

"Will do." I knew our only hope was Pasquale. He was in Angelo's villa and knew the layout. So, I called out, "Pasquale, let's sit down and come up with a plan."

Pasquale came over and said, "It's about time we finish this."

"I want you to make a drawing of everything you remember about the villa. Every entranceway way onto the grounds, and the best way into the house."

"I'm not an artist, but I can do that. I can even show you where the men are stationed outside."

"How many are there outside the villa?"

There are five men, one at the rear door, one at the front, and one at the side door. There are two men at the gate too. You can't see the gate from the front entrance. There's usually five men inside."

"Okay, how do we get onto the grounds?"

"There's only one way onto the grounds; through the front gate."

I looked at Pasquale, "They'll see us and have plenty of time to attack."

"Not if the power is killed. The main power for everything is by the side of the house, it's fed by a line on a pole about a half-block from the gate. All we have to do is kill the power."

"Are you nuts?" I snapped at him, "I know nothing about power lines on poles."

"Don't worry, Rico used to work for the power company in Bari, he'll kill the power."

"Then what?"

"First, I need a calendar."

"Why a calendar?"

"None of this will work if there's a full moon out." I had a calendar brought to him. "Great, no moon tomorrow night. When the power goes down, it will be completely black, that's when you knock out the two guards by the gate."

"Okay. How do we open the gate if the power is already cut?"

"I have been here a few times when the power went out, the gate and doors on the villa unlock. So,we just push them open. All the locks are electrical, so, they'll all unlock."

"When the power goes out, won't the men inside come out?"

"The power goes out a lot. So, the men are used to it. They stay where they are. One thing though, the generators will turn the emergency power on. But, we'll have a good ten minutes before that happens. We'll need to get in, split up, and take out the guards without firing a shot. Once you're in the house, the shooting will start. You better be ready."

"Who do you think we are, Delta Force?"

"This is the only way, Joey."

Giuseppe spoke up, "I know a way to take out the guards without shooting them."

"How, Giuseppe?" I asked.

"I have a cousin that lives about five miles from here; he will have what we need."

"What's that?"

"Tranquilizer guns." he offered with a grin. "He puts wild animals to sleep so he can tag them, I'll get three guns and some darts from him."

"Giuseppe, you're amazing. It'd be great if you can get them. One more thing; Rico won't get back in time. He'll be a half a block away."

"He'll be back; he uses a timer to shut down the power. I know he can do it, because that's how I was able to get away when Angelo found out I called Augie to warn you."

"Well guy's, we have a plan, not a great one, but nevertheless a plan. Make sure you have enough fire power and ammunition."

I walked over to Giuseppe and whispered to him, "I don't know how this'll turn out, so, would you and Alfredo stay here with my family? If I don't make it back, please see that they get to the airport."

"We will, Joey. Are you sure you don't want us to help you?"

"I'm positive. You and your son have done more than enough. I don't know how to thank you. I am eternally in your debt."

"Thank you, Joey. I am going to my cousins to get the dart guns."

"How long before you get back?"

"It'll take me about an hour."

"Okay, once you're back we'll have dinner and then we can all rest up for tomorrow night."

When Giuseppe came back he had four tranquilizer guns instead of three. I asked, "Why four guns? And why are they pistols?" I thought they were going to be rifles."

"Pistols are for up close. You'll need three men to put down the guards by the gate and the front entrance, and two men to take out the other guards. Don't forget, you only have ten minutes."

"Good thinking."

The next day we all just sat around and went over each detail of the plan. We were ready. Janet came over to me and asked, "Are you sure this plan will work, Joey?"

"Of course, I am. Don't worry everything is going to work out. I'm leaving Giuseppe and Alfredo here with you guys."

"Why?"

"Just a precaution, I want to keep my family safe. I have to talk to Alessandro, I'll be back in a minute." I went to Alessandro's office and told him I am leaving Giuseppe and Alfredo with my family. If I don't make it back would you help them get to the airport?"

"It will be my pleasure. "But, I have a feeling you will make it back."

"Thanks for the confidence, Alessandro."

"Well, Joey, I'm a firm believer that good triumphs over evil."

"I sure hope that's true, Alessandro."

"Just think positive, Joey. Think positive."

Chapter 14

We arrived in Bari around nine and parked our car in a secluded area that Pasquale showed us. The power pole Rico had to climb was fifty feet in front of us. I asked Rico, "Can you set the timer for ten o'clock?"

"No, the longest I can set it for is fifteen minutes."

"Okay, that'll have to do. We can wait here until it's time. In the mean-time get your gear on. I'll tell you when to climb." We waited about forty long minutes, continually watching for anyone that might pass. "Okay Rico, set the timer. Meet us fifty feet from the gate on the right side. As soon as the lights go off you and Pasquale take out the men at the gate. I will take care of the man at the front door, Justin you take the rear door and Gino the side one."

Rico climbed the pole, the rest of us, under cover of trees and bushes, worked our way toward the gate. Pasquale reminded us of the cameras, "Stay behind the trees and bushes." We stayed on the right side of the gate and behind the trees and bushes. Five minutes before the lights would go out Rico showed up.

It was the longest five minutes I could have ever imagined. Then suddenly, the lights went out. Pasquale and Rico walked right up to the gate, knocked the two men out with the tranquilizer, and pushed open the gate. I ran in and took out the man at the front door, Gino and Justin went to their positions and did their jobs. Everything was going fine until the generators kicked in sooner than they were supposed to. We must have been caught on the security system, men started coming out of the front, side, and rear of the building. I heard shots from the side and rear. I quickly changed to my piece as three men came out of the front door. I shot the first man and the two behind him started shooting at me. That's when Rico and Pasquale started shooting. I ran to the side to help Gino out. There were two men dead and three rushing Gino. I opened fire and shot two of them, Gino shot the third.

The shooting stopped in the rear of the building, I didn't know if that was good or bad. We rushed into the building and saw Rico and Pasquale shooting their way into the living room, I saw at least six men down. I figured Angelo brought a lot more men than we anticipated. Gino and I were now shooting men down as they were coming out of rooms. When I ran out of bullets I hid and reloaded. I spotted another gun from one of the men that was down and picked it up. We were shooting two guns at a time while we kept hiding, rolling and sliding on the floor. It kind of made me feel like I was in an old western shootout. Finally, they stopped coming. Gino and I looked around and saw that there were at least fifteen men that the four of us had taken down. I looked at Gino and asked, "Do you see Angelo or his wife in this mess?"

"No, I don't."

Pasquale chimed in, "They're probably hiding in the basement."

"Gino!" I shouted, "Check on Justin! I'll go down to the basement with Pasquale and Rico." We went into the basement but didn't see anyone. "There's no one here Pasquale."

"Oh, they're here alright. There's a secret door somewhere. The three of us started searching for a doorway that looked like part of the wall. Pasquale said, "I think I found it." He pushed on the shelving and it started opening. Pasquale yelled out, "Come on out, Angelo" There was no answer.

Rico came over and pushed Pasquale aside, shoved open the shelving and went inside. Shots rang out, I ran in and saw Rico on the ground, Angelo was lifting his gun and I shot him, he went down. Pasquale was right behind me and saw someone coming out from behind a large filing cabinet and, fired his gun. I turned and saw Carmine hit the ground. He was still breathing and I asked, "Where's your mother?"

Carmine looked at me, smiled and said, "You'd better get to your family and laughed." He stopped smiling, let out his breath, and didn't take another.

I turned to Pasquale, he was helping Rico get up, "How is he?"

He'll be okay. I heard what Carmine said. We need to get back to Alessandro's."

We went back upstairs and I saw Gino, "Where's Justin?"

Chapter 14

He's sitting on the couch. He's been hit twice, but not that bad."

"Okay." I said. "We need to get to Alessandro's fast, Angelina's on her way there to kill my family."

Gino asked, "What about Angelo?"

"He's dead. Before we leave I need to call Alessandro and warn him of Angelina." I told him what transpired, he assured me he would not let her or anyone get near my family. "Okay, put Rico and Justin in the back seat and let's go."

Before we got in the car Pasquale said, "I have a friend who can fix Rico and Justin when we get to the hotel."

"That's great, they certainly need it."

We took off racing toward Alessandro's hotel. Pasquale knew the shortcut, so he drove. It was around midnight and the roads were practically empty, so we were back at the hotel in less than two hours. As we were walking toward the hotel I asked Pasquale, "Could you stay with Rico and Justin?"

"Sure thing, just be careful. In the meantime, I'll ask my friend to get over here pronto."

I nodded and Gino and I went into the hotel. I walked over to the front desk and asked, "Is Alessandro here?"

"No, he's with your family, Mr. Toranetti."

"Thank you." I looked at Gino and affirmed, "We beat Angelina here. I'm sure she'll be here soon enough."

We went to my room and Janet came running over, her eyes were bright with tears, and her arms were up in the air and ready to latch on to me. "Thank God your safe!" She hugged me and wouldn't let go. "I love you, Joey, can we go home now?"

"I wish we could. Angelina got away and is on her way here. Gino and I will handle it. How are all of you?"

"Your father isn't feeling well, Rocco is nervous about you too. Where's Justin and Rico?"

"They're hurt. Pasquale has a friend coming over to attend to them."

"How bad are they?"

"There not too bad, just losing a lot of blood." I looked over at Alessandro and asked, "Can you take them to a safe place?"

"Yes. I have a place outside of Naples."

"Okay, I want everyone to go with Alessandro. Dad? Are you going to be okay?"

"Yeah, I just need to drink a lot of water and rest. I'll probably need another blood transfusion when I get home."

"Are you sure? We can take you to the hospital now if we need to."

"I'm positive. I've felt this way before. I know what to do."

"Now, everyone, go with Alessandro. Alfredo, Giuseppe, stay with them, Gino and I can handle this.

"I'm not going anywhere; I'm staying right here with you. Just give me a gun."

"I'm not going to argue with you. This is not up to debate. Just go with Alessandro."

Angelina and her two body guards walked into the lobby of the hotel, her actions screamed trouble. She approached the front desk and told them, in a foreboding voice, "Give me the room and location of the Toranetti family!"

Loretta, the front desk manager, responded with a quiver in her voice, "I can't do that, but I can call them for you."

Angelina took out her gun and shot into the wall behind Loretta and whispered, "The next bullet will be in your pretty little head!" The people in the lobby started running and screaming.

Loretta gave her the room number. As Angelina walked away Loretta called the room to warn us.

The phone in the room rang, I answered. The woman from the front desk on the other end was crying hysterically, "What's wrong?" She asked to speak with Alessandro. I handed the phone to him and said, "She's hysterical!"

Alessandro asked, "What's wrong Loretta!?" She told him what happened.

"What is it?" I asked.

"Angelina and her two goons are on their way."

"Get them out of here, Alessandro, including my wife."

Alessandro opened the second bedroom and herded my family in there. As soon as they were safely tucked away, the door of our room was kicked in. Two men came in shooting at anything and everything. Gino and I were on the ground and opened fire on them. They went down immediately. That's when

Angelina came running in, using an automatic rifle, she sprayed the room with an expertise that surprised me, up and down and then side to side. Gino had rolled to his left and me to my right. As she sprayed her bullets I opened fire and hit her square in the chest, she went down and Gino came running out and shot her in the head. She was dead. We could hear frightened hotel guests screaming and running around in a panic. I went into the bedroom, "It's over."

Janet came running out crying. She didn't say a word just held on to me, crying. "It's okay honey. It's all over now." I looked over at Alessandro, "I am so sorry about all this. I sure hope no one else was hurt. I will gladly pay for the damages."

"No need, Joey, I have insurance."

"What about your business and reputation?"

"I've been through this before. We'll survive. Do you and your guys need a ride to the airport?"

"Thank you, Alessandro, but no. We have to go back to Rome first."

"Why do we have to go to Rome, Joey? Janet asked.

Inspector Falcone has my passport. I can't fly without it."

Pasquale came to our room, looked around and saw Angelina and her men lying on the ground and said, "Well, I'm glad that's over!"

"Where's Rico and Justin?"

"They're in the car all bandaged up."

I turned to Alessandro, "We need to get out of here before the cops get here."

"Alfredo. Take the back roads out of here." Alessandro said.

Chapter 14

Alfredo looked at me and said, "Let's go, Joey. I can hear the sirens getting closer already."

We left in Alfredo's car and Pasquale left with Rico. I yelled out the window to Pasquale, "Thanks to the both of you. If you get back to Brooklyn look me up."

They yelled back, "We will."

We took off toward Rome and them to … who knows.

Chapter 15

We arrived at Giuseppe's villa early the next morning, ate breakfast, and I called the airport to make reservations for the day after I would get my passport going to New York. I was informed that there were plenty of seats left on the morning flight. So, I booked the flight for all of us. We would depart at ten o'clock. Alfredo said he would take us at seven-thirty.

I then called Augie and told him that the situation was handled, "That's great to hear, Joey. "Are they all gone now?"

"Yes. We're flying back tomorrow.

"Call me when you get in."

I asked Alfredo to take me to see Inspector Falcone. When we arrived, I asked the person at the desk to see Inspector Falcone. He recognized me and picked up his phone and told someone on the other end, "Mr. Toranetti is here." Looking directly at me he stated, "The Inspector will be right out," and he pointed to the bench by the wall.

Chapter 15

We sat and waited for the Inspector. It was about fifteen minutes before he came to greet us. Mr. Toranetti, how are you?"

"We are doing well."

"Have you enjoyed your stay in Italy?"

"It was remarkable, thank you.

"I have to ask you something, Joey,"

"Sure Inspector. What is it?"

"Well, I heard a rumor this morning."

"What might that be?"

"It seems that Angelo Scarapino and his crew were found dead at his villa in Bari. Do you know anything about it?"

"When was this?"

"Yesterday."

"Really?"

"Would you know anything about it?"

"How would I know anything about it, I was in Naples yesterday."

"I also heard that Angelina, Angelo's wife, was found dead in a hotel near Naples with two more men. I was told the room was full of bullet holes."

"Wow, that's unbelievable. Did they catch them?"

"Not yet, but they are still investigating the matter."

"Well, I hope they find them. By the way, how is Officer Alissi doing?"

"He's doing great. It's amazing how he is not as timid anymore."

"I'm glad to hear that. I'm here because I need my passport. We're flying back to New York tomorrow."

That is great news. I am glad you had such a wonderful stay. Will you be coming back soon?"

"Not for some time Inspector. It's been a pleasure." We shook hands and headed back to the villa.

When we returned, I announced to everyone, "I would like to take all of you to dinner tonight. You pick the restaurant since I don't know any here."

Giuseppe indicated, "That is not necessary, Joey."

"Yes, it is Giuseppe, I want to take this opportunity to thank each and every one of you for your support. Without you I would probably not be here. So, what restaurant would you like to go to?"

Giuseppe spoke up, "La Carbonara in Monti. It has been in business for over thirty years."

"Do we need reservations?"

"Yeah, but I know the owners and they will get us in."

"Great, La Carbonara it is."

"Can you set it up for seven, o'clock?"

"Sure thing."

We arrived at La Carbonara around 6:30, as we pulled up to the entrance we noticed the restaurant was in the middle of a large four story building. The building itself was very old but in decent shape. It was founded in 1906 and is still owned by the same family. The entrance is on the bottom floor in the middle of the building. A single door with a plain glass panel in the middle provided entry. There were varnished wood side panels around each side of the door with plain glass in the middle of each panel.

When we entered, we were met with alcove shaped walls that made you feel like you were walking into a cave. In the middle of each alcove were two tables for two. On each wall was a large board that people could write on, there were hundreds of signatures. Wine bottles lined the shelves on the upper part of the walls. There were tables for four in the middle of the restaurant. All the tables were set with attractive place mats, black cloth napkins with silverware perfectly placed at each setting.

When the waiter came over I told him, "This dinner is on me. My friends, order whatever your heart desires." Janet sat next to me. My father and brother sat on either side of us. Across from us were Alfredo, Giuseppe, Justin and Gino. We all ordered drinks and when they arrived, I stood up and made a toast. "We have been through a lot in the last couple of weeks. We have dealt with an evil that tried to outwit and destroy us.

If it weren't for you and your support, I would not have made it through this ordeal alive. I thank you, from the bottom of my heart. Salute!"

Everyone called out, "Salute!" We all sat down, ordered appetizers and our dinner. We all talked about the last couple of weeks and what our plans for the near future held. I rose from the table and exclaimed, "My friends, tomorrow, myself and my family will be going back to Brooklyn. We'll never forget your kindness and support."

After we ate dinner I turned to Giuseppe and acknowledged, "This restaurant is absolutely the best place I have ever eaten. The food was outstanding and the service impeccable. Thank you."

When we arrived back at the villa we finished packing our belongings. I looked at my family and expressed my feelings, "I am very thankful that you're all okay. I love you all. Thank you." We all hugged and back slapped each other. "Now we need to get some sleep. Alfredo is taking us to the airport at seven-thirty."

I was up by six and Alfredo was in the kitchen making espresso and coffee, "Good morning, Alfredo."

"Good morning, Joey. Did you sleep well?"

"Sure did. I can't wait to get back home though."

"I can certainly understand that. Are all your bags packed?"

"Yes. They're by the stairway."

I have borrowed a stretch limo so you will be more comfortable. I will start packing the car."

"I'll help you."

As we were loading the luggage I asked Alfredo, "Do you have my bill? I must owe you some money."

"The only money that was owed is what I laid out, and your father has given me a check for that already."

"Really, he didn't tell me. I hope he gave you some extra?"

"He did, I refused the extra amount. I told him, friends do not accept extra. He was upset, but wrote a new check."

"Alfredo, you are a really good friend. I hope you can come to Brooklyn one day for a visit."

Everyone came down, ate breakfast, and had some coffee. "Okay," Alfredo exclaimed, "It's time to go." We all piled into the limo and headed to the airport.

Chapter 16

We arrived at the Fiumicino Airport in Rome around 8:15 entrusting our luggage to the porters. Alfredo left to park the limo and we agreed that he would meet us at the check in. As we were waiting I noticed a few police officers entering the terminal. That's when I spotted Inspector Falcone with another officer approaching us. The two officers grabbed me, one on each side, holding fast to my arms, and pulled me out of the line and towards the exit. "What's going on?" Janet and the family tried to get to me before I was whisked out the door, but the police stopped them.

The officer that was with Inspector Falcone advised me, "Mr. Toranetti, I am Inspector Caprizio from Bari. You are under arrest for the murders of Angelo and Angelina Scarapino."

"Are you nuts? I didn't murder anyone! Falcone, what's going on?"

Inspector Falcone looked at me, shook his head, and stated, "They have a witness."

Chapter 16

"Whoever it is, is lying!" Just then my brother, who was able to get closer to me, called out to me, "Be quiet, Joey. Don't say anything else!"

Looking over my shoulder I called back, "Tell Janet and everyone to get on the plane. I'll be okay. You come with me."

Rocco walked over to Inspector Falcone, "I'm Joey's brother Rocco. I'm also his lawyer. Where, are you taking him?"

"They are taking him to the Questura in Bari."

Alfredo saw the commotion. Dumbfounded, he came over to Rocco and asked, "What happened?"

When Rocco told him, Alfredo exclaimed, "That's crazy! This is a setup for sure! Make sure your family gets on that plane, then come with me."

As the polizia were escorting me out of the airport I saw Janet trying to get through to me. The last thing I saw was my brother leading the whole family back into the line and Janet crying. I knew Rocco would have a hard time with Janet, but, I knew he could be very persuasive.

Once everyone boarded the plane Rocco met up with Alfredo by the pickup area. "Where are we going?"

"To my father's house. You'll need his lawyer's help to deal with this."

Reluctantly Janet boarded the plane and sat in the middle of Gino on the aisle and Tony by the window. Justin sat directly behind them in an aisle seat. You could tell Janet was about to explode, her face had turned a deep crimson and she was squinting so hard that her eyes and forehead were creased with wrinkles. Tony looked over at his daughter-in-law and understood exactly how she felt, "Janet, he'll be fine; Rocco is with him and will get him home."

"Dad, I need to be with him. I can't go home without him."

"Little Joey, needs you also."

"I know Dad. But, I have to help Joey first." Janet jumped up and squeezed past Gino yelling to the stewardess, "I'm getting off this plane." The stewardess was just starting to close the door Janet looked at her and said, "Please, let me off this plane." She looked and reopened the door.

Tony yelled over to Gino, "Go with her" Gino quickly strode to the doorway and disembarked following silently behind Janet. Justin started to get up and Tony told him, "Sit up here with me. I'll need your help."

Spotting a security guard, Gino asked, "Where can we get a cab?"

"Down the escalator one flight, and go outside; the taxi stands are there."

"Thank you." When they were outside they looked around for the taxi stand and spotted Rocco getting into Alfredo's limo. "Rocco!" Gino shouted out, "Wait for us."

Rocco turned, looked, and muttered, "What the hell? What are you two doing here? Why aren't you on the plane?"

Gino yelled back, "Long story." They all climbed into the limo and headed to Giuseppe's house.

Chapter 16

Alfredo pulled up to his father's house and everyone exited the limo. Giuseppe watched as the limo pulled up. He opened his door mystified as to why Joey's family was at his home. "What happened? Why aren't you on the plane to New York?"

"Joey was arrested at the airport," Alfredo explained.

"Arrested! For what?"

"The murders of Angelo and Angelina Scarapino."

"Are they nuts? Why now? Was it Inspector Falcone?"

"They have a witness. He was arrested by an Inspector Caprizio from Bari."

"Who's this witness?"

"We don't know, Dad. We need to help Joey. Rocco is Joey's lawyer, but he can't practice here. Can your lawyer help?"

"Of course. I'll call him." Giuseppe walked over to Janet, "We'll get Joey out of this."

With tears in her eyes Janet uttered, "Thank you."

"Where did they take him?"

"To the Questura in Bari."

"Rocco, my lawyer's name is Andrea Cortano, I will have him meet you in Bari. "When did the polizia leave with Joey?

"It's been about an hour."

"Okay. Since Falcone was there, I'm sure they had to go back to his headquarters in Rome to fill out paperwork. So, change cars and take Rocco and the rest of them to Bari. Now. You should arrive around the same time they do. Andy will meet you there."

At the Questura in Rome, Inspector Falcone, with Inspector Caprizio, questioned me. "Joey, what happened in Bari?"

"Inspector, I'm not trying to be a wise guy, but, I refuse to answer any questions without my lawyer present."

Falcone looked at me with a sad expression and pronounced to Caprizio, "Here's the paperwork you need to sign to take the prisoner." Falcone looked at me and voiced, "Good luck, Joey." Caprizio signed the papers and took me back to his car and we headed to Bari.

Chapter 17

It seemed like only minutes had passed when we approached Bari, and I was brought into an interrogation room at the Bari Questura.

The room was dark and gloomy, with an obvious two-way mirror. I knew someone would be watching and listening to whatever I said or did.

After sitting alone in the room for a while, the door opened and Inspector Caprizio entered, "Hi Mr. Toranetti, welcome back to Bari. You are here for the murders of Angelo and Angelina Scarapino."

"I didn't murder anyone."

"My witness says differently."

"Your witness is a liar"

"I have someone who wants to see you."

"It better be my lawyer"

"It is not your lawyer."

"Who is it?"

Caprizio opened the door. A man backed into the room and told Caprizio to shut the mike and the camera off. When he turned around I was in shock. There, in front of me, stood Carmine. He was still alive! I was too shaken to say anything. I just stared at him. "What's the matter Joey? Seen a ghost?"

"I don't understand; how is it you're still alive?"

Carmine laughed, "I have a neurological disorder called Narcolepsy. It's a sleep disorder. When, I get stressed I can go into such a deep sleep that sometimes, you'd think I was dead. It's called cataplexy. This is when a person becomes paralyzed and can't move. His or her vital signs are small or none for a short time. They can hear and see everything, but can't respond. So, I'm not dead, but, you will be, soon. Just think, I will do what my family couldn't and take over their business.

"So, you set me up to kill them for you?"

Yes, but you are very hard to kill—especially at the restaurant. I thought for sure we had you there."

"So, you put yourself in danger to implement your plan. That's sick."

"I figured if it worked, I'd be out of the misery I was in with my parents. Good luck getting out of this, Joey." He turned and strode out of the room.

Caprizio came back into the room and said, "Wasn't that a surprise?" He had a file in his hands, dropped it on the table and started. "Okay, Joseph Toranetti, let's get started." I just stared at him. "For the record, what's your full name?" I didn't answer him. "Answer the question Mr. Toranetti!"

"Is my lawyer here?"

"Who's your lawyer?"

Chapter 17

"Rocco Toranetti."

"I never heard of him. Is he a relative?" Again, I didn't answer him.

"Answer the question."

"Is my lawyer here?" Caprizio picked up his file and storming out of the room, quickly turned and came back, "Just so you know, in this country you don't have the right to see a lawyer before a hearing. I urge you to cooperate with me. I can keep you here for three days if I want. Think about it." He left the room.

Ten minutes later an officer opened the door and announced, "You lawyer is here."

Hi Mr. Toranetti, "My name is Andrea Cortano. I'm your lawyer. You may call me Andy."

"Who hired you?"

"Giuseppe Caladesse and your brother Rocco. They should be here shortly. I told the officer in charge to let your brother in when he gets here."

"Has the inspector questioned you yet?"

"He tried, but I wouldn't answer him."

"Very good. Do you know the laws of this country?"

"Not really. I just know that I'm being railroaded."

"Well, Caprizio doesn't have to let me see you. Since he agreed, I know, he really doesn't have a case. But, he can drag this out for years. So, let's you and I go over everything."

The door opened and in walked Rocco. "How are you doing, Joey?"

"I've been better."

"Joey, listen. Janet and Gino got off the plane."

"What? Why'd they get off?"

"You know Janet, and Gino wouldn't let her go alone,"

"Where are they now?"

"They're here with me."

"I want to see her."

"I know, but you can't right now. We need to get you out of here first. Talk with Andy. The laws in this country are not like ours."

"Andy, call me Joey. Before you ask me anything I want you to make sure the camera and mike are still off."

Andy opened the door and called, "Caprizio, turn off that camera and mike, now!" I had noticed the red light on the camera was on again after Carmine left. It blinked and Andy waited until the light went off.

"Okay, Andy. What do you want to know?"

"I need to know everything. Start from the beginning." I proceeded to tell him everything from the time I killed the Scarapino's godson, up to the incident at the Hotel Napoli.

"Okay. So, do you know who the witness is?

"I do, he came to see me before you arrived."

"Who is it?"

"Carmine Scarapino; their son."

"I thought you said he was dead?"

"I thought he was." I proceeded to tell Andy what Carmine said.

"My God, this guy must really be whacky to do something like that."

"Yeah. Now what?"

"How did he get in here to see you?"

"Caprizio let him in."

Chapter 17

"He's not supposed to do that. I'm going to try and get you out of here.

"I have one more question, Joey, and this one is important."

"What is it?"

"Did you murder Angelo and Angelina Scarapino?"

"I looked over at Rocco with an expression of help. Rocco responded, "Tell him the truth."

"No, I didn't murder anyone. I did what I had to do to protect myself and my family."

"Okay. That's great. Give me a few minutes with Caprizio."

Andy walked out of the room and over to Caprizio, and detailed what he had on Joey, "You have no solid evidence on Mr. Toranetti, only on a witness statement that is uncorroborated. You need to let him go until you have hard evidence."

"I have the witness. That's all I need."

"Speaking of the witness, why did you allow him to talk to my client in private?"

"I wanted to shake Mr. Toranetti up."

"If you don't let him go, you better be arresting him.

"I will arrest him in good time."

Andy now knew he was dealing with a crooked cop and stated flatly, "When you do, you better have more than just a mentally ill witness."

"Your client is a killer! And I will prove it!"

"Not today you won't, because if you arrest him, I will have the case thrown out completely.

If I arrest him without hard evidence, and only this witness who is a little off, and the case gets thrown out, I will, look like a fool. "Okay, he can go for now. I just need an address where he is staying."

"That's not a problem." Andy came back into the interrogation room and instructed, "Let's go Joey, we're leaving."

I got up and walked out, right into Janet's arms, "Let's get out of here."

We were getting ready to drive to Giuseppe's when Andy explained how the justice system works in Italy. *If I'm arrested, I could end up in jail for up to three years before I even go to trial.* "So, what do you suggest, Andy?"

"I think you should talk to Giuseppe about your options. I have to go see a friend. I'll call you in a couple of days. And, don't do anything foolish."

I looked over at Alfredo and said, "Let's get back to your father's place."

I hadn't told anyone other than Andy and my brother about Carmine yet. Just as I was thinking of how to tell everyone Janet looked at me and asked, "Do you know who the witness is."

You're not going to believe this, but it's Carmine." Janet was horrified.

Gino jumped in and with a look of horror on his face and stated matter-of-factly, "He's dead. We all saw him die."

I explained everything, even down to the set-up. "His last words to me were, *Good Luck getting out of this, Joey.*"

Janet regained her composure and asked, "What are we going to do?" I told her what Andy said about the laws in Italy. "This is turning into a nightmare all over again, Joey."

"I know, honey. Gino, as soon as we get back to Giuseppe's we'll need to talk about options with him. So, let's start thinking of some. Also, I'll need to call my father to let him know what's going on.

Andy Cortano left the Bari Questura and went to see his friend. Daniel Armani. Daniel is a retired police officer from the Polizia Municipale. "Hi Daniel. How are you?"

"Hi Andy. What a surprise. What brings you here?"

"I was in the neighborhood and thought of you."

"Sure, you did. What do you need?"

"I have a client that needs my help. To help him I need some information."

"What kind of information?"

"Do you know an Inspector Caprizio?"

"Yes. Why?"

"Is he, or should I say was he, on the Scarapino's payroll."

"I am pretty sure he was, but I can't prove it. Why"

"I heard a long time ago, certain cops would clean up certain crime scenes when it involved one of the families. Was he one of them?"

"I can't answer that, Andy. I really don't know. I wasn't in his circle."

"Can you say if you have ever heard of things like that?"

"I can say that."

"I am sure you heard of the shoot out in the Scarapino's villa, the other night."

"Yes, I did. What I heard was there were many bodies, bullet holes covered the whole interior of the villa, and, no guns were found. The polizia said they have a witness and a suspect. Is this your client?"

"I can't say. If you can get me some information on what I was asking, I would be very appreciative."

"I think I know someone who can help. His name is Alberto Rugini. He just returned from prison. He used to be very friendly with Caprizio. He may be able to help you."

"Where can I find him?"

"I'm not sure. I'll have to check around and call you."

"That'll be great. Here's my card, call me as soon as you can. And thank you"

Giuseppe gave me a big hug when we arrived, "Andy called and said you were on your way here. What happened? He couldn't tell me, and said that I needed to ask you."

I told him the whole story and pronounced, "We need to talk about our options, Giuseppe. The laws here are not like home. I need a plan."

"I know. The laws here can be severe. Right now, you had a long ride from Bari. Relax, clean up and we'll talk after dinner."

The last few days had been chaotic, relaxing is what we needed. I myself, am tired. As soon as I cleaned up I started feeling better. I knew I had to get out of this situation and couldn't wait to go over our options. We sat down for dinner, had some sumptuous wine, enjoyed some idle chatter, and had a few laughs. Once we finished dinner I asked, "Okay, what are my options, Giuseppe?"

"Depending on what Andy comes up with, you have three options. One, get rid of Carmine, two, leave the country, three, take your chances in court."

Giuseppe, you know none of those will work. If Carmine dies suddenly, Caprizio will claim I killed him. If I flee the country, there will be a warrant out on me and I could be extradited. And three, it will take upwards of three years before I even get a trial. What does Andy think?"

All Andy said was, he is working on another angle that could stop Caprizio and Carmine in their tracks. But, there is no guarantee. As soon as he knew, he said he would call.

"So, I guess, we wait.

Lying in bed, looking out the window, I watched as the sun rose over the horizon. I listened as the bells of the neighborhood church started to ring. The bells rang eight times. Unexpectedly, I caught the unforgettable aroma of fresh coffee brewing. I stepped out of bed and walked into the kitchen. Janet was getting breakfast ready. "Good morning, honey."

"Same to you, honey. Want some coffee?"

"Sure. What are you doing up so early?"

"I couldn't sleep. I'm worried, Joey."

"Don't worry, everything's going to work out."

"How can you be so sure."

"My father told me a long time ago to think positively. Negativity stops you from focusing." She walked over to me and hugged me tight.

Just then Alfredo walked in with a big smile and placed a bag on the kitchen counter. "Everything okay? I brought some pastries."

Janet smiled and said, "Thanks, Alfredo. "Now, I don't have to cook." We all laughed.

Alfredo asked us, "How would you like to get a gelato later?"

"Definitely," we both agreed.

We ate our pastries and decided to get ready for the day. While Janet was dressing the phone rang, Alfredo picked it up. "Hello? Oh hi, Andy. Yes, Joey's right here."

I grabbed the phone, "Hi, Andy. Have you found out anything?"

"Yes, I believe I have a way to get you out of this mess."

"How?

"I can't tell you yet. I still need to work it out. I need you to trust me on this.

I do trust you. But, I need to know what you have."

"The only thing I can tell you is, I can prove Caprizio is a crooked cop. I've set up a meeting with Inspector Caprizio, tomorrow at one o'clock. Just you, Rocco, and myself."

"Back in Bari?"

"Yes. If we leave at 6:30 we'll be there in time."

"I hope you're right, Andy."

"I know I'm right. It's just a matter of Caprizio, accepting it."

"Okay. Tomorrow morning it is."

Chapter 17

While I was on the phone, everyone had come into the kitchen. They all grabbed coffee and croissants, and waited for me to tell them what Andy had to say. When I put the phone down, I looked at everyone and yelled, "He's found a way!"

Janet ran over and grabbed me almost knocking me down. "Tell me what he has!"

"He can prove that Caprizio is crooked and has been taking money from the Scarapino family. That's all I know."

"That's great." Rocco exclaimed, "That shows complicity. That's a serious crime! Caprizio will lose his job and go to jail."

Giuseppe, with a big smile on his face said, "I told you he was good."

We all finished our breakfast and started getting ready for the rest of the day. While in our room Janet indicated her concern about the meeting. "What if this is a trap set up by Carmine and Caprizio to kill you, and your brother, along with Andy?"

"That's a great question, and it's typical of what Carmine might do. The meeting is at the Questura though. So, it's highly unlikely. But, I'll ask Gino, Alfredo and Giuseppe their opinions." Janet seemed to relax with that as she let out a sigh of relief.

When we went downstairs, everyone was waiting and chatting away. I saw that Giuseppe was finishing an Espresso and was about ready to leave. "Giuseppe, before you leave, I have a question that needs all of your attention," I told them the question Janet had posed and said, "I need your opinion."

Alfredo and Gino were on the same wave length, "Simple, Joey. We'll come with you, stay in the car, and make sure no one sneaks into the meeting."

Giuseppe said, "Joey, you don't have to worry about Andy."

"I'm not worried about Andy, I trust him. Who I don't trust are Caprizio and Carmine."

"Okay, I'll call Andy and tell him he'll have extra company, so he's not surprised."

"That'd be great. Let's go touring and get some gelato. It will help take our minds off things for a short while."

We needed to buy some clothes since our luggage had gone to New York. Stopping at some quaint shops we bought enough clothes for all of us to last at least a week. Rocco also needed a suit if we had to go to court. We found a small tailor shop that measured Rocco and in two hours made him a form fitting suit. Compared to New York, the price was fantastic for an Italian made-to-order suit. "Don't get it dirty, Rocco." Everyone laughed.

We went to lunch and then for our gelato. Alfredo took us to the same place we went to earlier in our stay, and it was as heavenly as the first bite.

When we returned to the house, it was close to dinnertime, but none of us were hungry. We all decided to get some sleep since we needed to leave early. Before I went to bed I asked Giuseppe, "Can you find out who is going to run the Scarapino's area."

"I'll let you know in the morning." I nodded and went up to bed.

Chapter 18

In the morning, I walked down to the kitchen and saw Alfredo coming into the house with a bag of pastries, coffee, and espresso. Giuseppe came over to me, "The families are splitting up the area."

"What about Carmine?"

"He's out."

"That's great, Thank you Giuseppe."

Andy walked into the house, without knocking, and came into the kitchen. "Is everyone ready?" We all nodded. "Alfredo, would you mind driving?"

"I don't mind." With that, we left for Bari.

The ride was long and very quiet. At some point I asked Andy, "Can you tell me what you're going to do?"

"Not until we're in the meeting. What I can say is I have two witnesses that will testify about Caprizio's dealings. So, just be positive and patient."

When we arrived at the Questura we asked to see Inspector Caprizio. "Whom may I say you are?"

"Andy Cortano."

The officer called, announced our arrival, and then escorted us to Caprizio'z office. We walked in and offered, "Good morning, Inspector."

"Buongiorno. I thought my office would be better than an interrogation room."

"It is much better, Inspector." Andy replied.

"So, Mr. Cortano, you asked for this meeting. What is this about?"

"I am going to make this simple. I want you to cancel this whole investigation against my client, Joey Toranetti."

The inspector started laughing, "You drove all the way across Italy to say that? Why, in the world, would I do that?" The inspector stared right at me. I stared back with a smile on my face. Then he looked at Andy and laughed.

"I'm glad you think this is funny, Inspector, but, I assure you that I'm not kidding."

"Tell me, Mr. Cortano, why should I even consider doing that?"

"Well, if you'll allow me to explain, without any interruptions, I will tell you."

Still laughing, the inspector said, "Tell me, Mr. Cortano."

"I will, just don't interrupt me."

"I won't. Proceed, but this had better be good."

"First, Inspector, I have two questions."

"Okay."

Chapter 18

"You'll be 62 next year, and you can retire with a full pension. Correct?"

"Yes."

"Okay. Here is the reason you need to consider what I've asked. I want you to know before I start I can prove everything I say." The inspector looked at Andy confused. "I know for a fact that you have been on the Scarapino's payroll for at least ten years."

The Inspector jumped out of his chair and yelled, "I have never been on their payroll!"

"I can prove it Inspector. Now, no more interruptions. You have been taking money and, cleaning up crime scenes to protect the Scarapino family for years. I have several witnesses that will testify to that." We watched as the inspector's jaw dropped, smile gone, a nervous twitch took its place as he stared blankly at Andy, baffled. "Shall I continue Inspector? Because I have a lot more. I can even tell you the officers you are working with."

"No! This, is blackmail!"

"No, Inspector. I call it leverage. If I should proceed with any of this, per the law, you will be disgraced, fired, lose your pension, and sit in jail for at least three years before you get a trial. So, what's it going to be?"

"Give me a minute I need to think this through"

"Think about what? Carmine? When you found him, he had been wounded, you thought he was dead, as you walked away he moaned and you knew he was still alive. What kind of a deal did he make with you?"

"He said he would give me a lot of money to keep quiet and arrest Joey Toranetti for killing his family."

"Well, Inspector, just so you know, Carmine, has lost everything. He has nothing, no money and no area to run. The families are taking care of that. So, are you done thinking?"

"Yes, I will do whatever you want if you won't tell anyone."

"I want a statement that Joey is no longer a suspect, and I want it now."

"Give me an hour and you will have it. There's a café across the street, I'll bring the paperwork there."

As we exited the Questura we signaled Alfredo and Gino and pointed to the café. We filled them in and they were ecstatic. We ordered food and waited for Caprizio. When he arrived with the paperwork, Andy read it carefully and said, "This will do. Thank you, Inspector."

"So, we have a deal, right?"

"Don't worry Inspector, no one will ever know."

Before we left the café, I asked to use the phone and slipped the owner a twenty. I called Giuseppe's. When he answered, all I said was, "Everything is great, let me speak to Janet. "Hey, honey, we're on our way back and now we can all go home."

She was so excited she started to scream, "Hurry back honey. I want you back here with me safe and sound. Just hurry."

"I'll be there soon. In the meantime, make flight arrangements for the three of us. First class."

While we were driving home I asked Andy, "How did you find all that information out?"

I talked to a few friends I know. They gave me a little and the rest was conjecture."

"You mean, you didn't have any proof? How did you know this would work?"

"I didn't have any proof. But, a guilty man would be inclined to think I did. I just had to present it in a convincing way. I must have been pretty close to his dealings. That's why I couldn't tell you what it was."

"What if it didn't work?"

"It did work, Joey. No more, what ifs."

"I don't know what to say, except, thank you. Rocco, I hope you learned something."

"I learned a lot. Now if only I can apply it to poker." We all laughed.

We arrived in Rome around eight that evening, Janet came running out to meet me, hugging, kissing, crying and hitting me. "Don't ever put me through anything like this again!" I started laughing and she hit me harder. We went inside arm-in arm where Janet had made our favorite dish, spaghetti with garlic and oil and Italian salad. We drank a couple of bottles of wine and rejoiced in our freedom.

"Janet, did you make the flight arrangements?"

"Yes, we're all set. Our flight is at one tomorrow, and as you requested, sire, we're in first class."

"Let's call my father and tell him the good news." My father was elated about the news. He would have a limo pick us up and we would celebrate. We couldn't wait to see little Joey, and get into our own bed. I looked at Janet, smiled and said, "Our vacations will be in America for a long time."

She looked at me and screamed, "Hallelujah!"

Trilogy: Books I–III

Print ISBN: 978-1937801526

Finally you can own the first three books in one. *The Other Brooklyn*, now available online and at a bookstore near you.

***The Other Brooklyn* also available in audio!**

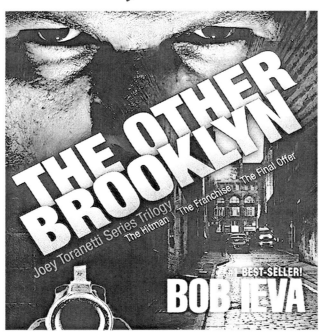

Audio ISBN: 978-1-937801-60-1

Books IV
The New Breed

Print ISBN: 978-1-937801-67-0

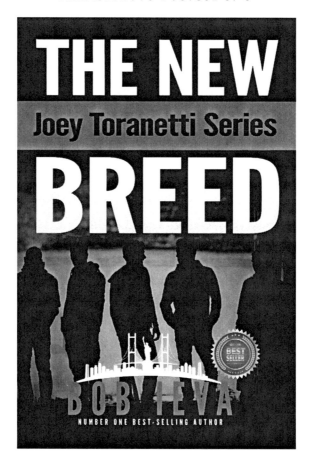

Watch for Book VI Coming Soon!

CPSIA information can be obtained
at www.ICGtesting.com
Printed in the USA
LVOW08s1239250717
542517LV00003B/534/P